Why her? Why now? Kyle asked himself.

It was a mystery, part of the larger one he was trying to solve—about his father and her mother, her grandfather and his grandmother.

Danger swirled around him like a fatal cloud of poison. But Megan didn't taste like poison; she tasted like honey, sweet and tempting.

He touched her and felt flames leap, part of him suddenly aching for things he couldn't name. He felt a tremor run through her, and he shuddered, lost to reason, as desire flamed higher for this woman, this lovely enemy who made him forget the past and ignore the future.

"It's hell," he heard himself say, "this wanting."

"Yes, I know," Megan answered feverishly. "To find this now, with you…"

"The enemy," he whispered, finishing the unthinkable thought.

Dear Reader,

International bestselling author Diana Palmer needs no introduction. Widely known for her sensual and emotional storytelling, and with more than forty million copies of her books in print, she is one of the genre's most treasured authors. And this month, Special Edition is proud to bring you the exciting conclusion to her SOLDIERS OF FORTUNE series. *The Last Mercenary* is the thrilling tale of a mercenary hero risking it all for love. Between the covers is the passion and adventure you've come to expect from Diana Palmer!

Speaking of passion and adventure, don't miss *To Catch a Thief* by Sherryl Woods in which trouble—in the form of attorney Rafe O'Donnell—follows Gina Petrillo home for her high school reunion and sparks fly.... Things are hotter than the Hatfields and McCoys in Laurie Paige's *When I Dream of You*—when heat turns to passion between two families that have been feuding for three generations!

Is a heroine's love strong enough to heal a hero scarred inside and out? Find out in *Another Man's Children* by Christine Flynn. And when an interior designer pretends to be a millionaire's lover, will *Her Secret Affair* lead to a public proposal? Don't miss *An Abundance of Babies* by Marie Ferrarella—in which double the babies and double the love could be just what an estranged couple needs to bring them back together.

This is the last month to enter our Silhouette Makes You a Star contest, so be sure to look inside for details. And as always, enjoy these fantastic stories celebrating life, love and family.

Best,
Karen Taylor Richman
Senior Editor

Please address questions and book requests to:
Silhouette Reader Service
U.S.: 3010 Walden Ave., P.O. Box 1325, Buffalo, NY 14269
Canadian: P.O. Box 609, Fort Erie, Ont. L2A 5X3

When I Dream of You

LAURIE PAIGE

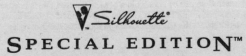

Silhouette®
SPECIAL EDITION™
Published by Silhouette Books
America's Publisher of Contemporary Romance

To my family (both in-laws and out-laws) for help with "best-laid plans." See you at the reunion!

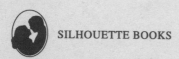

SILHOUETTE BOOKS

ISBN 0-373-24419-3

WHEN I DREAM OF YOU

This edition published by arrangement with Harlequin Books S.A.

Visit Silhouette at www.eHarlequin.com

Printed in U.S.A.

Books by Laurie Paige

Silhouette Special Edition

Lover's Choice #170
Man Without a Past #755
**Home for a Wild Heart* #828
**A Place for Eagles* #839
**The Way of a Man* #849
**Wild Is the Wind* #887
**A River To Cross* #910
Molly Darling #1021
Live-In Mom #1077
The Ready-Made Family #1114
Husband: Bought and Paid For #1139
†*A Hero's Homecoming* #1178
Warrior's Woman #1193
Father-To-Be #1201
†*A Family Homecoming* #1292
Make Way for Babies! #1317
***Something To Talk About* #1396
***When I See Your Face* #1408
***When I Dream of You* #1419

Silhouette Desire

Gypsy Enchantment #123
Journey to Desire #195
Misty Splendor #304
Golden Promise #404

Silhouette Yours Truly

Christmas Kisses for a Dollar
Only One Groom Allowed

Harlequin Duets

The Cowboy Next Door

Silhouette Romance

South of the Sun #296
A Tangle of Rainbows #333
A Season for Butterflies #364
Nothing Lost #382
The Sea at Dawn #398
A Season for Homecoming #727
Home Fires Burning Bright #733
Man from the North Country #772
‡*Cara's Beloved* #917
‡*Sally's Beau* #923
‡*Victoria's Conquest* #933
Caleb's Son #994
**A Rogue's Heart* #1013
An Unexpected Delivery #1151
Wanted: One Son #1246
The Guardian's Bride #1318

Silhouette Books

Montana Mavericks

The Once and Future Wife
Father Found

Fortunes of Texas

The Baby Pursuit

Montana Mavericks: Wed in Whitehorn

Cheyenne Bride
Outlaw Marriage

*Wild River
**The Windraven Legacy
‡All-American Sweethearts
†Montana Mavericks: Return to Whitehorn

LAURIE PAIGE

says, "In the interest of authenticity, most writers will try anything...once." Along with her writing adventures, Laurie has been a NASA engineer, a past president of the Romance Writers of America, a mother and a grandmother. She was twice a Romance Writers of America RITA finalist for Best Traditional Romance and has won awards from *Romantic Times Magazine* for Best Silhouette Special Edition and Best Silhouette. Recently resettled in Northern California, Laurie is looking forward to what-ever experiences her next novel will send her on.

THE WINDRAVEN LEGACY FAMILY TREE

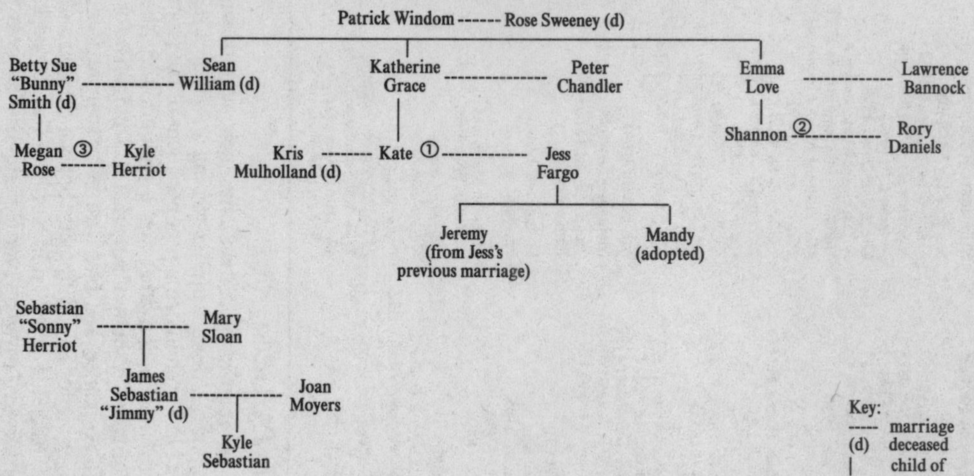

① —*Something To Talk About* (May 2001) SE #1396
② —*When I See Your Face* (July 2001) SE #1408
③ —*When I Dream of You* (September 2001) SE #1419

Chapter One

Megan Windom kept the smile on her face as she and her partner dipped and swayed to the rhythm of the first waltz of the wedding reception. Tears pressed close to the surface and she didn't know why. It was a happy occasion—the wedding of her cousin, Shannon, who was also her best friend, to Rory Daniels, another lifelong friend.

Turning her head, she quickly slid her gaze past her partner's angular, unsmiling face. Kyle Herriot, her enemy, son of the man who had caused her mother's death, met her brief look without a flicker of emotion in his eyes.

The fact that Kyle's father had also died in the sailing accident didn't mitigate the mystery of why Bunny Windom had been on his yacht or how and why she'd been knocked unconscious so that she hadn't had a chance to survive when the boat went down.

Sighing, Megan admitted that wasn't the only mystery in her life. At twenty-six, she had no memory of her first eleven years. It was as if her life had started the day of her mother's funeral.

That terrible day she recalled in vivid detail. The tears. The flowers. The overcast sky with lightning and thunder rumbling among the peaks of the Wind River Mountains. The terror and uncertainty as she watched them lower her mother into the ground—

"Bear up," Kyle advised. "The mandatory waltz of the maid of honor and best man will be over in another minute. It can't come soon enough for me, either."

He had a wonderful voice, husky and deep and resonant, like twilight and campfire smoke, like distant mountains and the wind through the cottonwoods. A lover's voice—warm and honey-smooth, with an undercurrent of intimacy shaded into the masculine tones.

But none of that was for her, because she was his enemy, too. Like the Hatfields and the McCoys, their families had been hostile even before the boating incident.

"I beg your pardon?" she said as if she had no idea what he meant. Her tone was calm, not at all in sync with the haunting melancholy inside her.

His lips curled up ever so little at the corners in a knowing smile filled with the acid sting of disdain.

"Being forced into my arms appears to be your idea of hell. You've sighed three times in the last minute."

"You overestimate your influence," she informed him with cool regard. "My sighs have nothing to do with you, only with…life."

She hated the hesitant note as she searched for a word that sounded innocuous, yet meaningful enough to account for her uncharacteristic moodiness.

Her enemy studied her, his thoughts unreadable in the depths of his gray eyes. A year ahead of her in high school, he'd treated her as if she hardly existed on the occasions they couldn't avoid each other, such as the Honor Society meetings. Kyle Herriot, football captain, had been vice president, then president when she'd been the treasurer.

Smart. Athletic. All around hero.

A shiver raced through her, a sinister warning of something she couldn't name.

Tonight he was incredibly handsome in a white dinner jacket and black pants, a boutonniere of pink-edged golden roses attached to the lapel. His black hair gleamed in the multiple lights of the candles spaced about the patio and rolling lawn.

June in Wind River, Wyoming, was unpredictable, but Mother Nature had chosen to be kind this year, so that the wedding reception could be outdoors rather than in the formal dining hall, cleared for the occasion. The night sky was star-spangled, the air crisp but warm enough for Megan to wear only a silk shawl draped over her long evening gown of golden silk.

Around them, other couples took to the floor, urged by the bride, who called out happy greetings to friends and family members as she danced with her new husband.

The tension eased from Megan's shoulders as skin-prickling stares shifted to other couples. A Windom in the arms of a Herriot was news in this part of the world.

Kyle led her in an intricate step. He was a wonderful dancer, as firm and decisive as a professional. Once he'd found out she could follow him easily, he'd surprised her with his skill. How odd, to know they *clicked* effortlessly on the dance floor when their chance meetings were filled with silent accusations and distrust.

Inhaling deeply, she caught the scent of his cologne and the clean smell of balsam shampoo and soap mixed with pine and cedar from the mountains. The aroma of the light floral perfume she wore wafted around them, too.

Confusing sensations swept through her. She was surrounded, surfeited by it all—the evening, the first stars, the beauty of the wedding, the happiness of the bride and groom, the complex emotions of the day coupled with the memories she couldn't erase and those she couldn't recall—

"Easy," the velvet-smooth voice murmured in her ear.

Kyle caught her close as her feet stopped moving,

causing them to stumble. She thanked him and tried, really tried, to smile, but her lips trembled with the effort.

"What troubles you?" he asked.

Surprised by the question, she answered honestly. "My father sat out here and cried the night of my mother's funeral. That was in June, too. Fifteen years ago."

The words tumbled out, startling her. She hadn't been consciously aware of them in her mind.

Kyle's expression hardened, but he said nothing.

"My room is up there." She nodded toward the window overlooking the patio. "I sat on the window seat and watched him, each of us alone and hurting, but I didn't go to him. I couldn't; it was too frightening, listening to my father weep. I've always regretted that."

"You were a child, what, nine, ten?" His tone was rough, not exactly sympathetic, but not hostile toward that child, either.

"Eleven. I'd just turned eleven in May."

A week ago she'd looked at the pictures of her eleventh birthday party. Cake. Ice cream. Friends. Her face lit with joy as she prepared to blow out the candles. A little over three weeks before her mother would go down in a sailing yacht belonging to this man's father.

"He should have comforted you."

"No." She understood her father's grief, the depth of it, the terrible, terrible pain of loss. He'd loved

Bunny Windom with all his heart and soul. She was sure of it.

Her partner said nothing else.

The dance ended in a grand flourish. Kyle swept her into a graceful dip, then twirled her around three times, stopping on the last beat of the music.

"Thank you. That was lovely," she automatically said.

His lips curled at the corners. "My pleasure."

After escorting her to the table where the wedding party had been seated, he deftly removed the bride from her new husband's arm and guided her onto the cleared dancing area. Shannon, looking as radiant as a dewdrop in sunlight, laughed as he executed a dramatic tango step with her.

The musicians immediately took up the tempo. Everyone stopped and watched the couple.

"Every woman's dream—a man who can dance really well," Kate, Megan's other cousin, remarked, taking the seat next to her husband.

"Hey, I didn't think I was too bad," Jess complained with good-natured complacency.

Jess was Megan's uncle, a virtual stranger who'd showed up last summer looking for clues to his sister's death. Bunny had lost track of her young brother—her stepfather had been a drifter—after she married and had always worried about his well-being.

"Well, for a cop with a limp, you're okay," Kate conceded, her blue eyes—the envy of every woman in the county—sparkling with love and humor.

A vise clamped around Megan's heart as she listened to the teasing between two of the people she loved best in the world. She really was emotional today.

Why? Because she was the only one left of the three cousins who hadn't found her true love? Was she so petty as to be envious of their happiness?

No. She really was pleased that Kate and now Shannon had found their soul mates. She approved of their husbands, Jess Fargo and Rory Daniels. She adored Jess's son from his first marriage and the couple's recently adopted daughter.

Hearing herself sigh again, she admitted it was her own low spirits, and a past she couldn't recall that bothered her today. She couldn't figure out why.

"Wanna dance?" thirteen-year-old Jeremy Fargo asked.

"Now that's an offer I can't refuse," she said with a warm smile. She was teaching him to ride and handle horses. They'd become good friends in the process.

For the rest of the evening, she danced and toasted the bridal pair with an enthusiasm that was sincere. Later, as she tired, her emotions became unreliable again.

She managed to stave off the odd and irritating nostalgia or whatever it was by refilling platters and keeping an eye on the caterers. When the food was replenished, she looked around for something else to do.

Seeing that everything was in order and the guests

happy, she relaxed and leaned against the wall, content to watch rather than take part.

"It's time," a deep, quiet masculine voice told her.

She glanced at Kyle with a question in her eyes.

"Rory wants to take Shannon home now. She has a headache, and he's worried. He doesn't want her to get overtired."

Shannon, a local cop, had received a head injury at Christmas and been temporarily blinded. Her vision had gradually come back, not all the way, but she could see.

The annoying, insistent tears pushed against Megan's control at Rory's consideration for his bride. "He's been so good for her," she murmured. Then, to her embarrassment, her eyes filled with tears, too many to simply blink away.

Kyle moved in front of her, concealing her from other curious eyes. His warmth surrounded her, oddly comforting but disturbing, too. She was aware of him, deep in her bones, in a way she didn't recall being aware of a man. It added to the welter of emotions that ruffled the even tenor of the evening.

"Does that bother you?" he asked, his harsh tones at odds with his kind actions.

Megan stared up at him.

"Did you want Rory for yourself?"

Her mouth dropped open, then she shook her head and managed a true smile. "I want the bride and groom to have all the happiness they deserve. I wish them the best."

He looked skeptical for a second, then shrugged. "How do we announce their departure?"

"We pass out the bags of birdseed." She slipped around his tall, lithe frame and pointed to a side table.

He helped her make sure each guest had a little net bag of seed to send the wedded couple off in a shower of blessings. When the bride and groom were gone, others began to take their leave.

Later, when all the guests had left, except for Kate, who'd stayed to help with the cleanup, Megan kicked off her shoes with relief.

"You don't have to do that," she scolded Kate, who was washing up a crystal bowl.

"This is the last piece. The caterers did a good job, didn't they?"

"Lovely." Lifting her left foot, Megan wiggled her toes. She was much more used to boots than heels—and preferred the more casual wear. Training horses and giving riding lessons was how she made her living. Horses were somewhat predictable. People weren't.

Kate dried the bowl and put it away. She hung up the dishtowel. "I hate to leave you here alone."

"I'll be fine." Megan managed another smile.

Her cousin wasn't fooled. Kate was seven years older. As a teenager, she'd often baby-sat Megan and Shannon. She'd been there when Bunny had drowned. Kate had been the rock that held steadfast for Megan then and five years later when her father had died in an automobile accident.

Their grandfather'd had a stroke shortly after his son died and lived the rest of his life in a wheelchair, hardly able to speak. It was all so sad—

Hot tears filled her eyes, startling her.

"Megan?" Kate said, concerned.

Megan grabbed a tissue and mopped her eyes. "I'm feeling terribly sentimental today. The wedding and all. Wasn't Shannon lovely?"

"Yes. Rory has been good for her."

Megan nodded.

"I can spend the night," Kate offered. "Jess took the children home. I have my car here."

Kate had brought over the roses that filled every vase in the house. The family green thumb belonged to her.

"Actually I prefer the quiet. It's been so hectic lately, I'm looking forward to not feeling compelled to talk to anyone or be social. Besides, I'm going out to check on a mare as soon as I change. If she's foaling, I'll be in the stable the rest of the night. You go home and take care of your family. You've done enough here today. Shoo."

"Okay," Kate agreed. "Come over for dinner tomorrow night. The guys have promised us fresh fish."

Megan had to decline. "I have late classes on Mondays." She walked her cousin to the driveway and waved her off.

It wasn't until Kate's taillights disappeared that she felt the loneliness close in on her once more. She stood at the top of the stairs, on the way to her bedroom, and listened to the silence of the old mansion that had sheltered several generations of Windoms.

Their grandfather, the family patriarch, had died during the spring, which was why Shannon had postponed the wedding until June. Now Megan was totally alone in the family homestead. It gave her an odd, unsettled feeling.

Like being the last of her kind.

Which wasn't true in the least. She had her two cousins, who'd been her friends and mentors all her life. She had her uncle, plus the two new cousins, Jeremy and Amanda. She knew everyone in Wind River, population one thousand, and the county. Besides her cousins and their families, other ranchers lived around the lake and along the county road. She wasn't alone, not at all.

After changing to a shirt, jeans and boots, she did go to the stable. The light flickered when she turned it on. If the electricity was going to go out, she'd better check the flashlight and fill the oil lantern. After doing so, she looked in on the mother-to-be.

The mare slept peacefully, waking only when Megan leaned over the stall. The horse rose and came to Megan, blowing gently into her ear and reminding her of the way a lover might tease during their lovemaking.

An image formed in her inner vision. Kyle Herriot. Now that her cousin was wed to his best friend, would she be forced to endure his company often?

Rather than recoiling from the idea, she studied it

from several angles, trying to assess her own reactions.

The past wasn't his fault. Nor was it hers. It was just there, a barrier as big as a boulder field laid down by the glaciers that had moved through these parts thousands of years ago.

Her grandfather had hated the Herriots because his fiancée had run away from him only days before the wedding and eloped with Sebastian "Sonny" Herriot instead. Megan wondered what had caused the flight.

A neighboring woman had once said her grandfather'd had a terrible temper during his youth, that he and his fiancée had had a fierce quarrel over her brother, who was in jail for cattle-rustling and needed a lawyer. Grandfather had refused to help. Megan supposed Kyle's grandfather had supplied the necessary funds.

Sad, what people do to their lives.

The hot rush of tears assailed her again. She hugged the mare and pressed her face into the rough mane, then drew away. "Go back to sleep, love."

Honestly, if weddings affected her this much, she was going to have to swear off attending them. She smiled, but the odd tumult inside didn't let up.

A warm, furry body wrapped itself around Megan's legs. Tabby dropped a mouse at Megan's feet.

"Thanks," she said wryly, bending down to pat the cat. "I think I'll let you keep the mouse. I hope this was the only one."

Satisfied that all was well here, she flicked out the light and headed for the house. On the deserted patio, she paused, feeling the rush of overwhelming emotion again.

Her father had wept here, alone in the night, for the wife he'd lost.

Megan sensed, if not his presence, then his grief, terrifying to the child she'd been at the time, utterly sad to the adult she was now. The soul of Sean Windom had died that night, although his body hadn't gone until five years later, when he'd had an automobile accident.

Drunk again, people had whispered. *Driving too fast.*

A sixteen-year-old at the time, she had vehemently denied he'd wanted to die. Now...now she wasn't so sure.

The thought seemed a betrayal of her father's memory. Pushing it out of her consciousness, she wondered why the past weighed so heavily of late. Since her grandfather's death in March, it had preyed on her mind and emotions.

The specter of cleaning out drawers and closets loomed over her. It was something she should do, but she dreaded it. Kate and Shannon would help, but she wasn't ready to face that task just yet.

Another shiver chased down her spine. Glancing once more around the patio, she slowly entered the house and felt its haunting emptiness. She walked upstairs, but instead of going to her bedroom, she went to the suite that had belonged to her parents.

She hadn't been back in here since she and her cousins had gone through and disposed of the clothing and personal items. Jess had searched the room last summer, sure he would find a clue to his sister's death. They had found only the usual things—photo albums, mementos from anniversary dinners, birthdays and the few vacations they'd had.

Gazing at the portrait of her mother, Megan was overwhelmed with love and despair and questions.

"Why?" she whispered, staring into green eyes that were so like her own. "Why were you out on that lake? Why were you with a man hated by our family? Why?"

The woman in the portrait returned her stare, the rose-petal lips caught forever in a soft, dreamy smile of perfect happiness, her belly flagrantly rounded with child.

The painting had been commissioned by her father for the couple's first anniversary. The unborn child was a girl. Herself. Megan Rose Windom, her parents' only child.

Closing her eyes, she tried to recall those early years. The happy times, she termed them. She had dozens of pictures of picnics, horseback rides and birthday parties to prove it. Her mother had been radiant in each of the early snapshots. When had their lives changed?

The past haunted her like a ghost at a banquet, demanding attention but refusing to show itself fully. Sometimes she got flickers of memories, but not enough…never enough to put the pieces together….

Turning abruptly, she fled down the hall to her room.

Dressed for bed, instead of climbing in the four-poster, she lingered with one knee on the window seat as she observed the moonstruck landscape sweeping down the pasture to the lake. Its surface was unnaturally still, splashed with pewter by the brilliant moon, reflecting the scattered clouds that drifted over the peaks to the west of the ranch.

The lake.

It looked beautiful, lying in a glacier-carved bowl, mysterious…treacherous.

The lake.

The place where a sailing yacht had crashed upon the rocks, and her mother, unconscious from a blow on the head, had drowned. An accident? The police report said so.

The lake.

It pulled at her as if the deep, cool water was a magnet of liquid metal, calling to her in nightmares that made her wake with cries of despair, fear eating her soul.

She blinked the sting of unwelcome tears from her eyes, her body tensed as if to run for her life.

The silvery surface of the water winked back at her, ruffled by a sudden wind blowing down from the mountain. From the cottonwoods by the creek, she heard the harsh caw of the ravens.

The ravens. Once they'd frightened her, too. The birds had cawed the night before her mother's death, or so it was rumored. She didn't remember.

What would it take, she wondered, to gather all the pieces of the past and put them in order?

Fear shuddered through her, but she ignored it. She wouldn't give in to terror like a child locked in a dark closet. The light of truth was what she needed to dispel the horror of her nightmares.

She would start in her grandfather's quarters. Soon. Next week. She would start next week.

It was a promise to the child who lived in the dreams that troubled her.

Chapter Two

Kyle Herriot held the door for his mother, closed and locked it, then set the alarm to go off if the door was opened again during the night. His mother'd had the security system installed fifteen years ago… shortly after his father's death.

"I'm glad that's over," she said, setting her purse on the marble-topped foyer table. "There's only the Windom girl left. When she marries, the name will be gone."

"Unless she chooses to stick with her maiden name." He followed his mother into the study. After pouring her a cordial of Riesling late harvest, he splashed an inch of brandy into a snifter and gazed out the windows that lined the western wall of the house.

The French doors opened onto a covered patio that looked out upon the mirror-smooth lake. One by one, the lights clicked off in the Windom mansion. He watched as headlights came on and the last vehicle in the circular drive sped away into the night.

Through the reflection in the glass, he saw his mother sit in her favorite chair, her eyes also drawn to the night scene beyond the windows.

"I've hated looking at that house," she said in musing tones. "For fifteen years. Since your father died."

He remembered the day as if it were yesterday. He'd been eleven, determined to go sailing with his dad, although he was on restriction due to some infraction of the rules. However, someone else had been with his father when he'd arrived at the boathouse on the lake.

Hearing an odd sound, he'd sneaked around the corner of the building and heard a woman crying. Sensing it would be unwise to butt in, he'd returned home, resentful that his plans had been interrupted due to adult problems.

"I wish I knew what happened that day," Joan Herriot continued, a thread of bitterness in her tone as always when discussing her husband's death.

"It was a long time ago."

She sighed. "I know."

They sat in silence for a while. Kyle saw the last light in the Windom house go off. Megan's bedroom, he assumed, from which she'd watched her father weep over the loss of the wife who had died with another man.

He resisted a stirring of pity for her, shaking his head slightly, denying the emotion. Like his mother, he had no sympathy for the Windoms.

His grandfather had hated them. He'd called Megan's grandfather an autocratic tyrant with an uncontrollable temper, a man who'd ruled the 5000-acre Windraven Ranch with an iron hand and little patience.

All that had changed after the old man's stroke, of course. It turned out the ranch had been in trouble. The three cousins had pooled their resources and saved the family homestead. He had to admire them for that.

Megan actually owned the house due to some convoluted inheritance from her grandmother—the woman Patrick Windom had married three months after Mary Sloan ran away from him and married Sonny Herriot, thus becoming *his* grandmother.

Now there was a tangled web, indeed. As far as he knew, no one had ever really known what had caused her flight.

"Are you all packed?" he asked his mother, trying to change the direction of his own thoughts.

"Yes," she said in a happier tone. "I'm not sure whether I'm growing more excited as the trip draws closer or more apprehensive. I keep thinking of a million things I should do here before I leave in the morning."

He laughed. "You've left a list of to-do's that will

keep me busy for the next two years. Enjoy your vacation. You've earned it.''

She finished her nightcap and stood. ''I can't wait to see all the plays I've read about. I need to get to bed if I'm going to be fresh in the morning for the trip.''

After she kissed him on the cheek and left, Kyle turned back to the house across the lake, his mood dark and thoughtful. Perhaps while his mother was on the month-long New York trip with a friend he would unravel some of the mystery surrounding his father's death.

With old man Windom's death back in March, there'd be no one to object if he nosed around on their side of the lake. Since he would have some time to himself, without having to worry about his mother's feelings, this would be the perfect opportunity to check out the sailing yacht that had never been brought to the surface.

Hmm, how hard would it be to bring it up?

That was something he could look into. Going to his office, he flipped on the computer, then went on the Net with instructions for the search engine to find information on boat salvaging.

Three hours later, he had most of the salient facts. Now all he needed was a bit of luck. And no interference from the ranch across the way.

Why should Megan object? The sailboat was abandoned. The insurance company had paid off and left the yacht on the bottom of the lake. According to what he'd read, it belonged to anyone who could bring it up. That's exactly what he wanted to do.

Climbing into bed in the wee hours of the morning, he heard the wind pick up, blowing down the mountain into the long valley of ranches and summer homes to the tiny town tucked into the far end. From across the lake came the sound of the ravens, crying out harshly from the cottonwoods by the creek.

There was a legend about the cawing of the ravens, something about true love going awry. But then, legends were always about lost loves or lost treasures or both.

He idly wondered if his grandmother had regretted her rash marriage to his grandfather and had wished she'd made up with Megan's grandfather. He knew his mother had never gotten over the hurt and humiliation of his father's being with another woman when he died, the two of them alone when the sailboat went down.

Or was scuttled.

He considered the possibility. Would an examination reveal what had really happened that day in June fifteen years ago? Or would it increase the mystery?

Tongues would wag if word got out about what he was doing, or attempting to do. While the site was at the other end of the lake, his neighbor across the way might get suspicious if she saw him going that way regularly, especially since he'd need to bring a compressor and a hundred feet of hose with him if he decided there was a chance of raising the yacht.

One comforting thought—it wouldn't be as difficult as raising the *Titanic.* He gave a cynical snort of laughter.

In his room, stripped and ready to climb between the sheets, he paused at the window, drawn again to the lake and the house on the hill beyond. Bathed in moonlight, the scene looked eerie and surreal, the house a gothic mansion of mystery and danger.

His body stirred as it had while he held Megan in his arms during the one dance they had shared. A horse trainer and breeder, she was slender, strong and lithe as a willow twig. The small calluses on her palms at the base of each finger said she was no stranger to work. He liked that in a person, man or woman.

Her hair was light auburn with lots of sun streaks, all acquired naturally. She had a few freckles on her nose. Her eyes were a mossy green outlined with charcoal gray, as inviting to a man as a patch of shade in a hidden glen.

Hunger pinged through him, reminding him of the feel of her in his arms—all bright warmth and feminine delight, enough to tempt a man into foolishness. He'd been surprised at the strength of the hunger she'd aroused. With an effort, he brought his thoughts and libido under control.

The expression in the verdant depths of her eyes had bothered him. Her smile had been forced. Something was definitely bothering the last single Windom cousin.

Perhaps she was jealous that Shannon had snagged

Rory Daniels instead of her. After all, the vet was her business partner in the breeding program. And Rory was "drop-dead gorgeous," according to all the women in the county.

Kyle was suddenly glad his old friend was safely married and out of the way. With a curse, he turned his back on the night scene and hurried to bed. He had no designs on Megan Windom. After all, they were mortal enemies.

That was a bit over-dramatic, but their grandfathers had definitely been enemies. He wasn't sure what had happened between their parents; however, he was positive his father hadn't been carrying on with another woman. It just wasn't in the man's makeup to be deceptive.

Or was he viewing the world through the rose-colored lens of youth? His own life had been happy and confident before the accident and underscored with bitterness and questions afterward.

What had happened that day on the lake? It was something he'd like to find out.

Megan woke to a chorus of chirrups just as the sun came over the far eastern peak. Snuggled under the comforter, she stayed in the warm bed and let her mind drift aimlessly.

No matter how warm the day, when night fell in the mountains, the temperature dropped into the chilly zone, sometimes near freezing. She'd always loved that early-morning crispness.

But today she was tired. Five hours of sleep hadn't

been enough to restore her body. Or her spirits, she admitted as a fresh wave of melancholy rolled over her.

However, Monday was a busy day. She had riding classes late that afternoon, plus the usual chores of feeding the stock and checking them over for parasites and pinkeye.

She threw the covers back. Only one way to deal with low spirits, she'd found. Get up and get busy!

After a breakfast of scrambled eggs, toast, cherry tomatoes and cantaloupe, she took an insulated mug of coffee to the barn with her. She was just in time.

The mare lay in the straw, her sides heaving in and out like a bellows in a blacksmith shop. Her water burst and spewed a geyser of salty fluid over the straw. The tiny hooves of the forefeet appeared.

Good. No breech birth to worry about. She wouldn't have to call out her partner and the local vet, Rory, who was now on the first day of his honeymoon. Although he and Shannon had decided not to travel, Megan would have felt terrible about asking for help.

Everything proceeded according to nature, though, and she chuckled as a very new filly tried to get her wobbly legs to cooperate so she could find her very first meal.

Megan and the mare helped, then Megan hung her jacket on a nail and set about cleaning up. After mucking out the stall, she spread fresh straw around and tossed a scoop of oats in the bin. Mother and daughter ate, then lay down for their first nap together. Megan got all choked up.

Pulling on the coat and grabbing the mug, she went outside to check the rest of her charges. She had three horses to train for recreation riding and one to correct for bad habits, such as biting a person on the leg when anyone tried to mount him. In addition, she was working with four yearlings to prepare them for the show ring.

She pulled in a deep breath. This was the life she loved. What more could one ask for?

The answer came swiftly. Her early memories, for starters. Contentment for another. With a wry grimace, she added wealth, happiness and Prince Charming. There, that should cover everything. Where was that genie in the bottle when a gal needed him?

Across the lake, she heard the drone of an engine. Glancing that way, she watched Kyle Herriot maneuver a small powerboat onto the placid water. He sped off toward the other end of the lake. Fishing, probably.

She recalled his mother was to have left early that morning for a vacation with one of her schoolteacher friends, another widow, so Kyle was on his own, too. She idly wondered if he could cook, a task she had little patience with.

Which reminded her, she needed to make a grocery list. The last month had been given over to wedding preparations and the refrigerator had gradually filled with special dishes as the big day drew near.

She'd eaten whatever was on hand and easy to fix, usually frozen entrées heated in the microwave oven.

She checked all the horses, repaired a fence, then headed back to the house. The temperature was rising rapidly. The afternoons were hot due to a high-pressure system sitting over this part of the state. She'd welcome a thundershower to settle the dust.

After freshening up, she took off for town in the ranch wagon, a list of chores in her pocket. The first person she saw at the feed store was Kyle. His fishing expedition hadn't lasted long.

Her insides clenched up.

She didn't like that a bit. He neither frightened nor attracted her, so why the emotional twinge?

"Good morning," he said when he saw her. He held open the door. No smile graced the planes and ridges of his face.

"Good morning. Did your mother get off on her trip okay?" she asked, pleased with the polite distance in her tone that gave nothing of her restless emotions away.

Her dreams had been filled with scenes she couldn't interpret—him and her, running from something, then her running from him while ghostly figures hovered ominously on the sidelines.

"Yes, considering she was afraid the ranch would fall apart without her watchful eye on things."

His rueful answer took her by surprise. So did the amusement in his eyes, which looked more silver than gray in the morning light.

"Mothers," she said, smiling with genuine warmth.

He seemed to stare at her mouth for a long minute before nodding. She turned down the first aisle of the store to escape him, then rubbed her lips to see if she had egg on her face.

She yanked out her list and hurried to the huge bags of feed. She might have known—Kyle was already there. He moved over so she could make her selections.

"Who's first?" the proprietor asked when he came to wait on them.

"He was."

"She was."

Megan glanced at Kyle in annoyance. "He was," she said firmly.

He shrugged. "I'm getting a hundred pounds of the special mix. I can handle it."

Megan watched him hoist a bag of feed as if it weighed no more than a five-pound bag of sugar. Muscles rippled in his arms and shoulders while others bunched in his thighs as he rose and slung the bag over his shoulder in one smooth movement. The owner dumped her order onto a wheelbarrow with a grunt, then headed out to her vehicle.

She gathered the rest of the ranch items on her list and went to the cash register. Kyle was there, asking about an air compressor. The store rented equipment to the locals as well as supplying them with crop seeds, stock feed and various medicincs and liniments.

"You two have got to quit meeting this way," the owner told them, laughing heartily at his joke.

Megan's smile was automatic, but her heart went into fast mode as she glanced at her enemy. His gaze locked on her mouth again and she recalled the way his eyes had roamed her face while they danced last night. His expression had been cold, but there had been something in those silvery depths....

Right. Dislike and suspicion.

She licked her lips and turned to Harry, glad to finish her business and get out of the store. After having her hair trimmed, she did the grocery shopping. By then, it was time for lunch. A meal at the local diner was the one treat she allowed herself when she had to come to town.

By rushing, she got a table just before a busload of senior citizens tramped inside. She watched them settle in, asking questions about the cooking methods of various dishes and the fat content, then ordering hamburgers and fries. The waitress, who had worked there just about forever, was the soul of patience, but she winked at Megan as she pivoted toward the pass-through to the kitchen.

Watching a frail old man, who looked to be around ninety, help his equally fragile wife to a seat, Megan wondered what memories they shared, the births and deaths, the unexpected joys, the deep sorrows—

"You expecting anyone?" a male voice asked.

She stared up at Kyle.

"Okay if I join you? The place seems to be full."

"Oh. Yes, that's fine."

He removed his Stetson and hung it on the back of a chair before taking a seat opposite her. He checked out the lunch special listed on the chalkboard. ‘‘You ordered?’’

‘‘Not yet. I’m going for the special.’’

The waitress came over and plopped down two glasses of water from a tray. ‘‘You know what you want?’’

‘‘The special with iced tea. Cornbread instead of dinner rolls,’’ he said after she ordered the same thing but with the homemade yeast rolls.

‘‘Got it.’’ The waitress hurried off.

Their table was an island of silence surrounded by a sea of babble, Megan realized. No conversational tidbits came to mind.

He had no such problem. ‘‘It’s going to be hot this afternoon. Again.’’

‘‘Yes.’’ She recalled the store. ‘‘You must have plans for some hard work.’’

Kyle looked a question at her. He watched the way the light picked out the red-gold tones of her hair and glistened like dew on her lips, which were outlined in a subtle color, then filled in with gloss.

She pressed her lips together.

‘‘Sorry,’’ he said, not meaning it. If he made her uncomfortable, tough.

‘‘For what?’’ She looked truly perplexed.

‘‘For staring. You have a tempting mouth.’’

He heard the hardness in his voice, but also the huskiness, the lover-like intonations. The tightening in his gut served as a warning; there was an attraction here...and it wasn't all on his side. There was awareness in her eyes, too. It made him angry, this unexpected hunger that throbbed in him.

What the hell was it about the Windom women that proved so irresistible to the Herriot men?

She ignored his statement. Looking straight at him as if he hadn't mentioned her mouth at all, she said, "But then, ranches always have lots of hard chores, don't they?"

"Usually," he agreed.

"Did you catch any fish this morning? You were out on the lake. I saw you," she added at his sharp look.

"Are you keeping track of my comings and goings?"

"Hardly. I was outside. I heard the motor. Sound carries across water."

He debated telling her what the compressor was for. The wreckage was on her side of the lake. Each landholder owned a section of the water that bordered their place. The Windoms, with the longest stretch along the waterfront, laid claim to the largest portion. But what he did was none of her business, he decided.

"No, no fish."

"That's too bad."

"I enjoyed the ride," he said, keeping his tone casual while he wondered if she'd seen where he went.

"My father always said that, too. He said sometimes catching a fish was an annoyance when all he wanted to do was relax and not have to work.''

Her laughter was unexpected, a gift like a perfect sunset after a hot, tiring day. It spiraled around inside him, then dipped into a secret, sensitive place.

Forcing his way past the strange sensations, he reminded himself it was her mother who had lured his father to his death. He wasn't sure how it had happened, but he would find out. He'd bring the sailboat up and maybe discover the truth....

The light in her eyes died. He watched her chest lift and drop in a sigh as the laughter faded.

''You're sad again,'' he said, feeling it in that secret place, ''the way you were last night.''

Her hand jerked, splashing several drops of water on the table as she lifted her glass. ''I've been thinking about the past. I don't remember—''

She stopped abruptly, her eyes darting to his, then away. He recalled adults whispering about the tragedy and shutting up when he came near. The sheriff had questioned him, of course, but he really hadn't known anything, except that he was the last person to see his father and Megan's mother alive.

For a second, he felt as he had last night when tears had suddenly filled her eyes, as if he needed to protect her. He wanted to gather her close and dispel the lost look in those beautiful eyes. He wanted to know this lovely, complex woman in a way he hadn't other females. Odd.

''You don't remember what?'' he questioned.

"Anything. Nothing of my past before my mother's funeral."

He'd heard the rumors about her amnesia. If that's what it was. "Does your uncle know about this?"

"Of course."

"It isn't generally known."

"My grandfather ordered my cousins and me not to discuss the incident with anyone."

"Did you and your father talk about it?"

"Some. Later. He told me not to worry about my memory, that losing my mother was a traumatic experience, and I shouldn't be surprised that my mind had blocked it out."

"Huh," Kyle muttered.

The hair prickled on the back of his neck. A lot of secrecy had gone on about this case. His mother, because she thought her husband was cheating on her. Megan's grandfather, because he was a proud, stubborn old man who wouldn't allow a hint of scandal to touch his family. And Megan's father, because...

Because he'd killed them and made it look like an accident?

It was a thought that had occurred to Kyle before now. But not one he wanted to discuss with the woman across the table from him.

The waitress brought the two specials. She plunked a basket of rolls and cornbread muffins on the table between them. Kyle wondered what other things he and Megan Windom would share before this adventure he was contemplating was finished. He had a feeling their lives would become entangled, and that was a dangerous thing.

The blood throbbed through his body, making him tense and heavy in certain areas, lighting fires he wasn't sure he could control. The path ahead was murky, an adventure into the unknown, but he was going to pursue it to the bitter end, wherever that turned out to be.

Chapter Three

Megan went through the usual rigors of the week. Horse-training actually meant training the owners, which was a lot harder than dealing with their mounts. On Friday, she controlled her impatience with an effort as she guided seven girls and three boys through their paces.

Kyle was on the lake. She'd heard the powerboat shortly after three and seen him heading out from the boathouse toward the narrow end of the lake.

It wasn't the first time she'd noticed him out in his boat. He'd been fishing every day that week, having acquired a great enthusiasm for the sport, it seemed. And he always went toward the narrows, the place where dangerous boulders and rocky outcroppings barred the way of easy cruising.

The place where the sailboat had gone down.

Suspicion sliced into the low spirits that plagued her. It crossed her mind that he might be exploring the wrecked sailboat. Why, after all this time?

Thinking of the tragedy reminded her she still had tasks to perform. Tomorrow she would definitely go through Grandfather's things and clean out his closet.

Or tonight.

Why put it off? This afternoon, as soon as the class was over. Yes, that's what she would do.

"Head him straight, Kathy," she called to one of her students, who couldn't seem to get any commands across to her horse. "Let up. You're holding him in too much."

The girl was afraid of all animals, yet her parents insisted she not only learn to ride, but to train for show-jumping. Megan worried about the twelve-year-old who was trying so hard to please the two most important people in her life.

The sadness hit her again as she thought of parents and what they did to their kids. However, her father had been wonderful after her mother died. He'd held her each time she woke from the terrible nightmares, confused about what was real and what wasn't. Each time, he'd assured her it was only a bad dream and that it would soon go away.

Shaking off the useless emotions, Megan headed inside as soon as the last lesson was over. After eating a quick sandwich and downing a glass of tea, she went to her grandfather's quarters, which had been a butler's pantry, herb-drying room and back parlor in the early years of the house.

The musky scent of closed rooms assailed her when she entered. She pulled back the drapes and threw open all the windows to let the fresh air roam through.

The parlor had been turned into a bedroom. The wall between the pantry and herb room had been removed, creating a combination office and library for her grandfather after he'd had the stroke and could no longer walk upstairs.

Megan paused, then went to the bedroom closet. Few clothes remained. Patrick Windom had stubbornly worn his ranch clothing until the jeans and work shirts had worn out, then he'd gone through the dress shirts and pants. The suit jackets had been donated to charity long ago. There was little to do but place the remaining items in bags for the dump or the church emergency supply.

The drawers and shelves took little time, and she was soon finished with the task. She stood at the office door, staring at the massive desk that had served several family patriarchs through the years.

Tomorrow, right after the chores, she would go through this room. Unexplained dread wafted through her. She didn't know what she was afraid of, but it was time to face those fears. She knew Jess would be interested, but she didn't intend to ask for his help. This was something she needed to do on her own.

If she discovered anything, she wanted to evaluate

the information first, then...then she'd make a decision.

The next morning, Megan woke at dawn as usual. She put on a pot of coffee, then, munching on an English muffin, headed out to start the chores. Saturday was livestock auction day, but she decided not to go. She didn't want to take on any more training chores just yet, although she made part of her living buying, training and selling Western riding horses.

In a field near the house, she waved to the farmer who leased their land. He was cutting hay, which would be stored for winter feed.

After feeding the mare, she let mother and daughter into the pasture next to the barn. Cattle roamed the meadows and rocky hillsides with their young ones. The sky was clear. The lake was still. All of nature looked peaceful.

Sitting on the rail fence, she studied the tranquil waters and wondered if Kyle was out in his boat again.

Probably not. The sun was barely up. She'd have heard the engine in the quiet of early morning. Gazing toward the section where the lake narrowed to a point and a creek flowed into it from the high mountain peaks, bringing down snow melt and glacial runoff, she considered an idea that had been running through her mind all week.

Why not investigate the wrecked sailboat?

Surely no one had a better right. Besides, she'd

read the police reports. She knew exactly where the wreck was.

Once she'd gone out there by herself and, with her snorkeling mask on, had been able to make out the lines of the craft on the rocky shelf beside a huge block of granite pushed into the lake by a glacier long ago.

Excitement pulsed through her. The water was icy cold in the depths, but it was bearable near the surface in the summer. She could stand the temperature long enough to dive down to the wreck and look it over, see what there was to see. Maybe she would discover something.

Or maybe seeing the boat would trigger her memory. That's what she wanted more than anything, to simply remember, to find the child she'd been and put her and the memories to rest.

The troubling sadness struck her again. It was as if her adult self felt sorry for the child she'd once been. She didn't understand it at all.

Leaping from the rail fence, she jogged to the house. There, she called Kate's number and asked for Jess.

"He isn't home," Kate said. "He and the kids have gone to Medicine Bow for the auction. They'll be gone all day."

"Darn."

She thought for a minute. Her two female cousins lived along a creek that ran into a shallow finger of the lake. Jess and Kate often took their kids for a cruise in the evening. They would surely notice any activity, even if it was at the opposite end of the long, narrow lake.

"Can I take a message?" Kate asked.

Megan took a deep breath. "I want copies of all the information he has on the sailboat that went down, all the photos and police reports. I'm going to—"

She tried to think of an explanation.

"Check it out?" Kate finished on a curious note.

"Yes."

"Sometimes," Kate said slowly, "it's better to let sleeping dogs lie."

A chill crept up Megan's neck. "I may remember," she reminded her older cousin. "Seeing the sailboat could trigger my memories of the past."

"The memories might not be pleasant, not all of them."

Kate was the nurturer in the family. She always considered the impact of events and worried about the consequences. Her concern warmed Megan.

"I know, but…I want to know."

"Even if you remember everything that ever happened to you, even if we discover all the facts, we still might not understand the why of it."

"It's something we all have to face," Megan said, resolute in her quest. "I'd just like to know what happened. The whys and wherefores I'll leave to those who want to speculate on them."

"It'll stir up old gossip, that's for sure."

"That's why I want to keep it quiet. Mrs. Herriot has gone on vacation for a month, so there won't be anyone around to notice. That should be enough time. I thought Jess should know what I'm doing.''

''Of course. He'd be upset if you left him out. Looking for clues to his sister's death was what brought him here in the first place.'' Kate paused, then said, ''Aunt Bunny was a wonderful swimmer. If she'd been conscious, she could surely have saved herself.''

The chill entered Megan's heart. ''That's what I'm thinking, too. I'll need to use the boat for a while. Is that okay?''

''I'm sure it is. Jess can bring it up to your dock when he gets in this evening, along with the police file.''

''Great. Thanks. Why don't you and the kids come up, too? We have a ton of stuff left over from the reception still in the freezer. I can drive you home later.''

''Okay. See you around six, maybe seven.''

After Megan hung up, she showered and changed to shorts and T-shirt. Going to her grandfather's study, she started on the bookcases first.

The ranch ledgers were stored there, dating from a hundred years ago and detailing the life of the ranch in terms of cattle sold or lost to storms, predators and disease, crops raised, including costs and selling price per bushel. Every penny earned and spent was recorded.

The records from the prior hundred years had been lost due to fire, her grandfather had once told her. The house had been rebuilt at that time.

Pausing, she studied the tatter of memory. She was sure the information had come from her grandfather before his stroke, but she didn't know when.

She went methodically through every ledger right up to the present and found nothing unusual. No notes tucked inside any. No confessions or incriminating information. She dusted the shelves and returned the cloth-bound records to their place. By late afternoon, she'd gone through the three glass-fronted bookcases.

Surveying the massive rolltop desk with its many nooks and crannies, she really doubted she'd find anything in it that might jog her memory of the past.

The sailboat was the key. She didn't know why she thought that, but she kept coming back to it.

Tired and dusty, she quit for the day. After washing up, she checked the time. Surprised at the lateness of the hour, she thawed wedding leftovers, little two-bite sandwiches of chicken and ham salad, which she ate along with string cheese and an apple for her supper. She put out some frozen pastry swans filled with whipped cream and several fruit tarts for Kate and her family, then put on a pot of coffee.

Hearing a boat motor on the lake, she looked out in time to see Kyle pull up to his dock and disappear into the attached boathouse. She frowned in his direction, wondering what the heck he was doing and how she could avoid him while she searched for clues.

Fear and anticipation ran through her as she thought of unlocking the door to her past. Kate worried that she would be hurt, but it was a chance she had to take.

A few minutes later, the old fishing dory that Jess and Jeremy had rescued from the barn and restored to running condition pulled up to the Windom pier. Amanda jumped out before anyone could help her, her brother hot on her heels.

"Mandy," he said sternly, "you wait up or else I'm going to pound you."

"You won't really," the five-year-old informed him with irrepressible humor. "Mom won't let you."

Jeremy grabbed her hand. "You're not supposed to run on the dock. You might fall in."

"I can swim," she said with righteous indignation.

"Yeah, and the Loch Ness monster might eat you, too."

"Ha."

Amanda obviously didn't believe in monsters. Megan smiled even as the unpredictable tears crowded her throat at the affectionate teasing. She wished their lives could always be as happy and carefree as they were at this moment.

Foreboding hummed through her, a never-forgotten melody that hinted at death and unspeakable grief.

"Hey, Megan, guess what?" Amanda demanded. "Larry Leighson lost his front two teeth. He looks yucky."

Larry had been Amanda's man of the moment prior to this misfortune. "It happens," Megan said sympathetically. "Next year your teeth will start falling out, too."

"I bet the tooth fairy leaves me a whole dollar. Larry only got two quarters and a book."

"Wow. That was pretty nice. I never got more than one quarter."

"Oh." Amanda paused, checked her front two teeth and looked disappointed that neither was loose.

Megan hid a smile as Jeremy rolled his eyes. She greeted Jess and Kate. "Thanks for bringing the boat."

"Here's the folder," he said, handing over the information she'd requested. "So you want to check over the sailboat? Are you going to try to bring it up?"

"Well, I'm not sure about that. I mean, how would you go about it?"

Jess pushed a lock of unruly hair off his forehead. "Use a compressor to blow air into the hull and force out the water. That's what we did on marine rescue."

Megan was startled by this information. "Kyle Herriot was asking about a compressor at the feed store last week."

Jess looked more than a little interested. "Hmm, maybe he's going to try to float her to the top. With two boats, you could probably pull her in to the dock if you get her up, even if the hole is below the waterline."

"Oh, really?"

This possibility hadn't occurred to Megan. However, it obviously had to her close-mouthed neighbor. Now all his ‘‘fishing’’ trips made sense. He was after the wreck, too, and she didn’t like his sneaky way of going about it.

But, in all fairness, his father had been involved. If he was searching, too, then maybe they should join forces. Later, when they found out the truth, or all that they could about the tragedy, then they could part ways and forget each other’s existence.

Uneasiness washed over her. Kyle Herriot might be a hard man to forget. Their lives were entangled on an elemental level that involved their families over two generations. Maybe it was unwise to add a third generation to the mix.

For the next hour, she and Jess and Kate discussed the known facts concerning the sailing incident, plus ways and means to bring the vessel to the surface so they could study it up close. Jess wanted to be in on the latter part.

Megan promised him that if she succeeded, he would be the first to know. After all, Bunny had been his beloved older sister, the one who had practically raised him while his mom had had to work to support the family. His father had been an alcoholic and drifter.

After driving them home in the old station wagon, Megan returned to her house. Its loneliness rushed out to greet her when she entered the door to the mud room off the kitchen. Seeing the envelope on the counter, she picked it up and hid it in a kitchen drawer.

The key to her past might lie in that envelope. She realized she was ready to face it, whatever it might be.

The air was hot and listless on Sunday afternoon when Kyle turned the key on the powerboat. The engine caught, and he eased out on the mirror-smooth surface of the lake. With the engine at half throttle—because he hoped not to attract his neighbor's attention—he pointed the bow toward the far end of the cool waters.

He wasn't having much luck in finding the wreck. He'd searched the dark depths in a grid pattern, but a whole week had been spent in futile exploration.

Had he known who'd done the original diving, he would look them up, but he didn't. He could ask the sheriff, who had been the investigating officer on the case at the time, but the sheriff might mention it to Shannon, a former cop, who would surely mention it to her cousin, Megan.

He didn't want any interference from the Windom side of the lake.

Following his grid plan, he slowed when he came to the boundary of the last search area.

"What the hell?" he muttered.

Another boat was three hundred yards away, anchored next to a huge slab of granite that jutted from the water like a monolith to some ancient god. Angling around, he glided over to it.

"Hey," he called.

His voice echoed off the cliffs at the edge of the

lake and came back to him. With an irritated curse, he pulled alongside the slab. He tossed the anchor out, then tied a line around a handy boulder. He climbed out of the boat and walked along the granite slab to the other boat that had a small motor mounted on the recently replaced transom.

Looking over the old dory for clues to its ownership, he spied a cooler and a backpack. Sneakers and socks lay on the bottom of the fishing boat. A long-sleeved shirt lay on the plank seat. They were on the small side.

Probably a boy exploring on his own. What was Kate's stepson's name? Jeremy. Yeah. Jeremy Fargo. But he'd never seen the boy out without other members of his family.

Where the hell was the person?

Bubbles preceded an answer to that question. A head broke the surface of the water. Through a snorkeling mask, Megan Windom's eyes locked with his.

She removed the mask. "Speak of the devil," she murmured, "and look who's here."

"What are you doing?" he asked, ignoring her snide attempt at humor.

Without answering, she kicked her way over to the slab, then tossed the mask and flippers out before climbing up on the granite. "Mm, this feels good. The rock is warm."

Heat pulsed through him when she stretched out and closed her eyes against the sun. She was dressed in a one-piece swimsuit, high-cut on the sides. Her legs went from here to forever, long, lean and shapely. There were faint tan lines at her ankles and high on her thighs.

The heat became an inferno. He was aware of the tight discomfort of his swim trunks under his jeans. The reaction increased his annoyance.

"You didn't answer the question."

She opened her eyes a slit. Shading them with an arm over her forehead, she studied him for a long minute. "I'm doing what you suspect," she said coolly.

He wondered if that was true. Without admitting anything, he drawled, "Then we're both out for a leisurely cruise of the lake."

"Right. The way you've been all week."

So she'd known of his prior trips. Damn. Looking into her frank and somewhat hostile gaze, he made an instant decision. "I'm looking for the wreck."

"The sailboat?" she said with only a slight questioning inflection.

"Yes."

"Why?"

He shrugged. "To reclaim what once belonged to my family. I'm thinking of restoring it."

"You want to study it," she corrected, her tone as icy as a winter wind off the mountains. Her gaze challenged him to deny it.

There was an honesty in her that he hadn't expected. It forced him to answer just as candidly. "The thought had occurred to me."

Instead of objecting, she became introspective. "Jess is interested, too. Bunny was his sister."

"Jimmy was my father. The boat was his." He figured that gave him first priority.

"Bunny was my mother."

"There is that," he conceded.

She was silent for a long minute, then said, "Okay, I'll work with you."

This was a development he hadn't foreseen. He didn't want any interference. "No way."

"It'll save you time."

"How?"

She smiled. "I know where the wreck is."

Glancing at the water, he returned the smile. "So do I…now. What brings you out here at this late date?"

"Curiosity," she said easily. "I want to see whatever there is to see."

He realized the same feelings drove her that drove him. But to work together? It was a volatile mixture in more ways than one.

"Why are you searching now?" she asked. "It's been a long time."

He decided on maximum honesty. "Your grandfather is gone. My mother's on a trip. I figured no one else would care or object to my prowling around."

"What are your plans?"

"Do some diving, locate the wreck and see what the chances are of bringing it up. The water is deepest here, around a hundred feet."

"The boat is on a shelf. It didn't go to the bottom."

That was news to him. He gave her a sharp perusal. "How do you know so much?"

"Jess and I studied all the reports. The sheriff's divers took some photos. Shannon got us copies."

"I see."

What he saw was more complications. He hadn't planned on anyone else horning in. He wished he hadn't been quite so open with his attractive neighbor. Working with her, if she really did insist on participating, was another twist he didn't need in his life.

"I'll get the photos to you."

"I'd rather you didn't."

Her eyebrows rose.

"I want to look the wreckage over first. Before we bring in anyone else."

Megan didn't tell him she already had the information, or that Jess already knew about Kyle's suspicious fishing trips. "Compressors are dangerous for a lone diver. You can inhale carbon monoxide and pass out, if that's how you're going to get air while you're underwater."

He was surprised at her knowledge. "I have air tanks. I used to dive a lot during my college days."

"Oh."

"I'd rather not broadcast what we're doing until we know more about it. I don't want my mother upset if I can prevent it."

"Were you going to hide the sailboat, assuming you bring it up?"

"We still have the boathouse. I'd put it there until

I had a chance to talk to her upon her return. I don't want to shock her…or the community,'' he added, warning her that he wanted to keep the quest strictly between them.

''I see.'' She stood and went to the dory. After pulling on the shirt, she turned to him. ''You'll need a wet suit to stay down any length of time. The water's too cold to stay in for more than fifteen or twenty minutes.''

He'd figured he could stand the cold long enough to do what he needed. However he had a buddy in California who would ship him a wet suit, if he needed one.

''So, do we work together and pool resources?'' she asked.

He couldn't figure out an argument to dissuade her. There was also the fact that she could observe his every move. Stalling for time, he nodded. ''Why not?'' he said.

But if he moved fast, he could get what he wanted and get the sailboat to the boathouse before she realized what was happening.

''You'll call me when you come out here?''

Suspicion was rampant in her expression. He smiled as guilelessly as he could. ''Sure. You're right. Two can work faster than one.'' He realized he'd been too cheerful when she frowned in distrust.

''I can hear any boat coming this way,'' she warned.

''So can I.'' But only if the wind was in the right

direction off the lake. She had the advantage of him on that point. Damnation.

Nodding, she untied the dory, tossed the line into the boat and hopped in with a push to start her off. In a minute she had the motor running and was headed toward home.

Releasing a deep breath, he stripped to his trunks and dived into the chilling water. That took care of the rampant hormones that plagued him in her presence.

He made it down to the wreck in a free dive, but couldn't stay long. She was right; the cold was mind-numbing, too dangerous for a lone diver to attempt.

So, he'd work with her as long as he had to…but whatever they found, the sailboat was his.

On Monday evening, after her last riding class was over and the chores were finished, Megan debated with herself, then picked up the telephone and dialed Kyle's number, after looking it up in the book. Her scalp prickled as she waited for the call to go through.

He answered on the first ring.

"This is Megan. I have the police photos and the file information, if you're interested in seeing them," she told him in formal tones. She was irritated with him.

There was silence on the other end.

"Hello?"

"I'm here," he said in that smooth voice that reminded her of summer breezes and long summer nights. "That was fast. I thought we'd agreed not to let others in on what we were doing until we knew more."

"I believe in acting once a decision has been made. As you apparently do, too. I saw you on the lake earlier."

Another pause. "I see."

"Did you do any diving this afternoon?" She wanted to let him know she was keeping an eye on him.

"No." His tone was a chill wind off the mountain. "I was checking out the rocks in the vicinity."

"I called you when I got information. I expect the same courtesy from you." She was cool and crisp, businesslike.

"Yeah, sure." He sounded distracted.

Maybe he had someone there with him and was impatient to get back to her. Feeling slightly guilty for bothering him and further irritated by the fact, she asked, "Do you want to come over tomorrow and see the photos?"

"No. I want to see them tonight. I'll be right over."

"Tonight?"

"Yeah. The moon is bright. I'll be over in the boat in about ten minutes."

He didn't ask if it was a convenient time for her. He just assumed it would be okay and hung up.

Fuming, she put on some decaf coffee. Although she wasn't feeling particularly neighborly, she still had about twenty pastry swans stuffed with whipped cream in the refrigerator. She'd offer him dessert.

After kicking off her shoes, Megan flicked on the dock lights, then sat at the kitchen table and waited. When she heard the sounds of an engine, blood pounded with unexpected ferocity throughout her body.

That was another concern to add to all the others. Nothing good had ever come of a Windom getting mixed up with a Herriot.

Chapter Four

Megan answered the door on the first knock. "Come on in. I've made coffee. Would you like some cream-puff swans?"

"Like those at the wedding?"

"Yes."

"Yeah, that sounds good. I forgot about dinner."

That information put her into a dilemma. As a good neighbor, she should offer him something to eat. Well, she certainly wasn't going to cook for him. With a grimace, she asked if he'd like some leftovers. "There's about a dozen of those little sandwiches left."

"Any with the ham spread?"

"Yes."

She placed all the remainders on a platter on the

kitchen table, put out a plate, pointed out the microwave oven and told him to help himself.

He did. When he'd finished, the finger sandwiches were gone, along with the pâté, stuffed olives and some kind of veal loaf, then he polished off the last of the cream-filled swans. He finished off the glass of milk she'd also offered.

"That was good. Thanks."

"Would you like a cup of coffee?"

"Please." He put his dishes in the dishwasher while she poured two cups of coffee.

She joined him at the table and removed the folder from the manila envelope. Laying it on the table in front of him, she said, "This is all the information Jess and I have collected from the official files and the newspapers."

"Nice to have relatives in the sheriff's office, huh?"

He didn't cast any particular inflection on the words, so she wasn't quite sure how to take the statement. Ignoring it, she was silent while he perused the reports. When he came to the photos, he studied each of them in detail.

It was a few minutes after ten when he finished.

"What do you think?" she asked, getting up to refill their cups.

"You were right. The sailboat isn't as far down as I thought. Maybe it won't be an impossible task."

"To float it to the surface?"

He gave her an appraising glance as if reassessing her intelligence. His expression was stony.

"Jess thought maybe that was why you wanted the compressor, to float the *Mary Dee* to the top. He said with the two motorboats, we could probably pull her in."

"Oh, he did, did he? Did you discuss this with anyone else that I should know about?"

"Well, Kate was here."

His lips thinned to a straight line. She returned his scowl with no expression whatsoever. Slowly his frown changed from anger to...she wasn't sure what.

"You drive me crazy when you do that," he at last said.

"What?"

"Look at me like that. Your eyes are fathoms deep and mysterious, like a mossy pool hidden in the woods. You're good at disguising your thoughts."

She blinked in mild shock at his words. "So are you."

His gaze continued to move over her, from her eyes downward to her mouth, where he lingered for a long moment, then a quick flick along her shirt, then back to her eyes.

Heat slid gently up her neck and into her face. Her breath went jerky until she forced herself to breathe deeply several times. She stared at him, into eyes that seemed to be charcoal rather than silvery-gray tonight.

All at once she was aware of the hour, the silence of the house and the fact that they were alone in the mansion.

A shiver ran over her like a sweet wind that set

the cottonwood leaves to shimmering. She felt hot and cold at the same time.

"Damn," he said softly, resentfully.

She sucked in a deep breath.

"This is a complication, isn't it?"

He sounded as if he spoke more to himself than her, but she answered honestly. "No." At his quick glare, she added, "I mean, why should it be? We're adults. We can control our actions."

"Can we?"

He rose and came to her. She watched him warily, not sure what was happening, or how she should react.

"Let's see," he said, taking her arm. A challenge.

She stood and let him draw her close, not quite touching, but aware, oh, so aware, of his tall, lean body an inch away. "You're right," she said quickly. "It is a complication. It could be."

"It is."

His voice had dropped a register, becoming a husky whisper. He bent forward slightly until his lips were on a level with hers. She held very still.

When he touched her mouth, every nerve in her body clenched in surprise as an electric arc went right through her. She fought the feeling, then she relaxed. She merely had to be objective about this.

The kiss wasn't bad; it wasn't bad at all. There was resentment, but it was coupled with gentleness and control. There was a desire to punish, but also a need to nourish. He was a complicated man.

His lips were smooth, with a decisive firmness she

would have expected from him. They were warm and supple as he moved across her mouth as if experimentally tasting each separate corner, then the middle. He didn't ask that she participate, so she waited.

When he lifted his head, she opened her eyes—when had she closed them?—and looked into his, held by his gaze.

"I could grow used to this," he murmured.

His words seemed so whimsical, so unexpected from him, that she smiled. He moved his hands from her shoulders to her back in a caress that brought his chest in contact with hers. She had to open her mouth to breathe as her throat closed up.

He gave her an intense perusal. "Don't do that."

"What?"

"Breathe. Talk. Look at me like that."

"Then don't kiss me."

She wasn't sure it was her voice that had spoken. Like his, it was husky and deeper, quiet, but with an edge of desperation as she tried to think.

His brief laugh was cynical. The sound rolled over her in subtle waves of the odd sadness mixed with longing. She understood then that he desired her...seriously...that the darkness in his eyes was passion...and something else.

Longing? Denial? A sense of betrayal?

Did he feel as betrayed by the physical reaction as she did? "We're enemies," she said, reminding herself as well as him of that fact.

"Yes."

When he kissed her again, she was ready. She met

the kiss, letting her lips fuse with his as the moment became hotter, the need more demanding. She felt his hunger in the clenching of his hands on her shirt and the undeniable reaction of his body against hers.

Her body answered, becoming soft, pliant, receptive. She wanted this man. This man, her enemy.

For a minute she let the kiss take her, following where the hunger led, then she drew back and shook her head.

"No."

"No?" he questioned.

His hands, big hands with strong fingers and callused palms like hers, stroked down her spine, one after the other. It didn't take much imagination to picture them caressing her in other ways, other places.

She stepped back, jarring the chair. The low screech rent the silence that stretched between them.

"You're right," he finally said and released her. "This is a road that has no place to go."

He picked up the folder, stuffed the info inside and slid it back into the envelope. "I'll take this with me if you don't mind. I want to study it some more."

Nodding, Megan waited for him to leave.

At the door, he paused. "Sure you want to work with me on this? I promise I'll keep you informed of my findings. You and Jess."

"I'll be free from around ten until two tomorrow," she said in a level voice. "I'm going out. I have my own boat."

The withdrawal was complete, the heat replaced

by an unshakable coldness when he spoke. ''Yeah, I know.'' He opened the door. ''See you at the rocks. Ten sharp.''

She watched him go without speaking. When his boat was across the lake and out of sight, she locked the back door and slowly went upstairs. Her legs were actually shaky as she climbed the steps. She felt as if she'd been through a test of endurance. She wasn't sure if she'd won or lost.

Kyle dropped anchor beside the huge granite slab left thousands of years ago by the glaciers that had carved the valley through the mountains. For a moment he thought of the forces that had shaped the land, then of those that shaped human lives. Both were relentless and unpredictable.

Like that kiss last night.

No more of that. He'd given himself that advice about a hundred times that morning. Maybe if he said it often enough, he'd begin to believe it. She was susceptible to the passion between them, too. Maybe, if he were lucky, she wouldn't show up.

The sound of a small engine dispelled that notion. In a few minutes, she tossed out her anchor on the other side of the boulder from him. ''Good morning,'' she said brightly.

Her eyes were clear and guilt-free.

''The sleep of the innocent,'' he remarked. His own sleep had been troubled by images of him and her and other vague, slightly threatening shadows in the background.

Her stance became wary as she stepped out on the huge, fissured slab of rock larger than an average home. "What does that mean?"

He shrugged. "I'm going down to look things over. I'll attach a line and buoy to the wreck to make it easier to locate. Give a tug on the line if anybody shows up."

Megan nodded. He was aware of her watching him check out the regulator on the scuba equipment. She got out her snorkeling fins and mask. "I wish I could go down, too."

He slipped the tank on over his jeans, T-shirt and long-sleeved work shirt, the nearest thing he had to a wet suit. The mountain lake was incredibly cold. He figured he'd last for ten to fifteen minutes at the most.

"You can try out my gear later, after I see that it works okay," he told her.

"Good. Thanks."

"What are you planning on doing with those?" He indicated her mask and fins.

"Watching you."

That's what he'd figured. The lake was clear as crystal since there'd been no severe storms of late to stir it up. A dime dropped into its depths would be visible for at least thirty feet. The wreck was around sixty feet, he estimated. Its outline was discernible if one knew exactly where to look.

Easing into the water, he drew gently on the air supply, which he'd refilled yesterday. Everything seemed to be okay. He clipped on the weight belt and dropped into the cold depths, taking the buoy line with him.

The wreck was where the police report said it was, straight down along the sheer drop-off of the rock slab. No wonder she'd found it so easily. He tied the line to the rail, then did a circle of the boat.

Although a layer of silt clung to the railings and all surfaces, the name, *Mary Dee,* after his grandmother, was still visible in gold letters on the aft of the vessel.

His grandfather had loved his Mary, a gentle woman who had told Kyle stories from her girlhood, of ranchers and miners and trappers who had come West to find their fortunes. She'd said he'd find his treasure someday, too.

At the time, he'd dreamed of pirates' loot and pieces of eight. Grown up, he'd realized she'd meant treasures of the heart. In the silent coldness of the water, he felt his own mortality and had a strong impulse to *hurry* before life passed him by.

Dismissing the thought, he cursed silently when he spied a huge boulder and smaller ones lying on the forward deck, which canted into the dark upthrust of granite.

Completing the tour, he checked the buoy line, then headed for the top. Megan was holding on to the buoy, her eyes visible through her mask as she watched him come up.

He wondered what his father had felt for Megan's mother, then cursed again as his head broke the surface.

"What's wrong?" she immediately asked, climbing onto the granite slab and removing the mask. "Didn't you get down to the sailboat?"

"Yes."

"The news isn't good," she concluded.

"There's been a rock slide, most of it onto the deck of the boat. That'll have to be removed before we stand a prayer of raising it."

"I know. We had a small earthquake a few years ago. Wyoming and Montana are among the top five or six states for seismic events in the U.S."

"Thank you for that important bit of trivia." He climbed out on the rock, which felt blessedly warm.

"Your lips are blue," she said. "The water's too cold to stay down for long."

"Tell me something I don't know."

"You're grouchy." Her face was perfectly bland as she imparted this additional bit of knowledge, but her eyes sparkled with impish humor.

He grimaced in irritation.

"The past bothers you as much as it does me," she said more slowly, as if just figuring this out.

Her tone was so sympathetic, it had him gritting his teeth. She was in that one-piece suit again, looking like a water nymph come to life. The temptation was too great after the kiss they'd shared. He wanted another one.

"You bother me," he said, then reached for her, hooking a hand around her neck and holding her head in place.

Surprise danced over her face, then his mouth

touched hers and he closed his eyes as heat pushed the chill out of his bones.

Megan opened her mouth to protest, but the words died as he slipped his tongue between her parted lips. His lips were cool and damp against hers, but in less than a minute they were warm…warm and demanding.

She sensed the struggle within him in the turbulence of the kiss, going from hard to gentle to something like harsh but not really. *Desperate.* Perhaps that was the word.

It was the way she felt inside—desperate and needy. She wrapped his cold, wet body against hers and tried to share her heat as confused emotions slipped into and out of her consciousness faster than she could identify them.

At last he pulled free, his hands on her shoulders holding her off. ''Was this the way my father felt?'' he asked in a near-snarl. ''Was your mother this much of a temptation to him, so that he couldn't resist?''

The words struck deep within her, to the place of darkness and terror and nightmares.

''Did she lure him to his death like the sirens in myth, making him forget the wife and child he'd left at home?''

Megan scrambled to her feet, moving backward up the slanted rock face. ''My mother loved but one man. That was Sean Windom. She wasn't involved with your father or anyone else. She hated her stepfather for cheating on her mother. She would never betray a trust.''

He slipped out of the scuba tanks, then his wet clothing. Her breath hung in her throat. It was with relief that she saw the trunks he'd worn under his jeans. She looked away with an effort.

''Then what was she doing on a sailboat with another man?'' He stood and took a menacing step toward her.

''I don't know, but it wasn't because they were having an affair. My parents loved each other. I know they did.'' She heard the desperate denial and knew, in her heart, that she wasn't sure at all.

''I used to think that. Until recently. Life can put too much temptation into a man's path.'' His lips curled into a disdainful smile at her indignant anger. ''You don't know anything,'' he added cryptically.

''*You* were the last to see them. Tell me what you saw,'' she demanded.

''Them standing on our dock. Her crying. My father saying soothing words. I couldn't hear what they were.''

''Was he touching her? Did they have their arms around each other? Were they clinging to each other like lovers?''

''No. They were just standing there, not touching. At least, not when I looked around the corner of the boathouse. She put her hands over her face. His hands were clenched into fists. He looked mad. She looked miserable. That's when I decided I'd better get the hell out of there.''

The tension left her. "You see? It was nothing."

"Nothing?" He stared at her mouth. "Yeah, nothing."

He turned away. Hoisting his scuba equipment into his boat, he secured it under the bow deck.

"Are you giving up?" She couldn't believe he would quit just like that.

"For today. I need a wet suit to stay in the water for any length of time. I have an old college buddy from California who'll lend me one of his."

"Oh." She couldn't hide her disappointment.

His laugh was sardonic. "Did you think we'd bring her up today and solve the mystery once and for all?"

"Not really. I guess I'd hoped it would prove an easy job, but nothing ever is, is it?"

"No."

She gestured toward the fishing boat. "You said you would show me how to use your scuba gear so I can go down and see the boat up close."

Kyle was silent for so long she assumed he'd refuse, but he plopped down on the warm rock. "All right, but there isn't much to see. I have some lunch. Let's eat first."

"I want to study it," she said stubbornly.

He said nothing else, so she took his silence for assent. Getting the cooler, he unpacked chicken salad sandwiches, pickles and sweet peppers. He handed her a bag of chips and a soda. "Help yourself."

During the meal, she experienced a return of the melancholy that had never really left her since her grandfather's funeral in March. Glancing at Kyle, she saw his gaze on the mountains, his thoughts fathoms deep but unreadable to her scrutiny.

That he blamed her mother for his father's death was ridiculous. Her mother had been too open, too honest and kind to hurt others with irresponsible behavior.

An ache grabbed at her heart. She'd thought his father must be the responsible one, but what if both of them were wrong? What if there was some other explanation for that day? What if…?

"The truth," she murmured. "That's what I want to know. Just the truth."

"All of it." His eyes locked with hers, a challenge in them, as if he thought she'd hide the facts if they weren't to her liking.

Drawing a deep breath, she nodded. "All the truth, no matter what it is."

"Yes."

They had made a pact, she realized.

Chapter Five

Megan woke with a start. Sitting up, she looked at the bedside clock. Five o'clock in the morning. Thursday. She rubbed her eyes and sank back on the pillow.

The nightmares. Again.

In her dreams, she heard a child crying. The sound echoed through her consciousness, blocking out logical thought. She put her hands over her ears, but the soft, helpless weeping went on and on.

The hopelessness of the child in the nightmare bothered her the most. It was as if the young girl saw no end to her misery, as if she'd been condemned to live forever in this particular hell she occupied.

The problem was, the dream never detailed the scene before the child started weeping. Shannon, with a Ph.D in psychology, had given Megan several suggestions on handling the haunting dreams.

One, she could teach herself to wake up when the nightmare started and order herself not to dream about that. Two, she could give herself a conscious command to dream of more pleasant happenings. Or three, she could decide on the ending she wanted for the dream.

There was another possibility. She could order the dream to start with the inciting incident, the event that had made the child weep, then follow it through to the end.

The familiar terror rippled over her.

Shannon had warned her there could be something so frightful in her life that the child couldn't face it, but that, as an adult, she would know what to do and be able to handle it...if she could reassure the child that it would be all right to remember.

She hoped that was true.

Snuggled under the covers, she tried to go back to sleep, to force herself to face the trauma, but she was wide awake now. She got up, dressed and went downstairs to put on a pot of coffee. Across the lake, a light gleamed in the Herriot house. Kyle must be up, too.

Leaning against the counter, she rubbed a fingertip over her lips and recalled the exact feel of his lips on hers. To desire her enemy seemed a betrayal of all she believed in, such as family ties and loyalty.

The attraction was mutual, but he seemed to dislike her, even blame her, for it. His ties to his family were as strong as hers.

Hearing an engine outside, she went out on the patio. Kyle was tying up at her dock. She walked down the lawn to the lake front.

"I talked to my friend in California. He's sending two wet suits. He thinks his wife's will fit you okay. He's also sending her air tanks. They'll be here within a week."

"That's very nice. Please thank him for me." After his curt nod, she asked, "Would you like some coffee? I was just going to have some."

"Coffee sounds good. Until the wet suits arrive, I'm going to try to move some of the smaller rocks, then figure out a way to shift the big one when we get the suits."

"Good idea."

He followed her up to the house and into the kitchen. Seeing him cover a yawn when he sat at the table where she indicated, she thought he looked tired.

"Have you been up all night? Your light was on when I came downstairs."

"Yeah. One of my best brood mares had a difficult delivery. She's never thrown a breech birth before."

"Is she okay?"

"Yes, but we lost the colt."

"Birth and death," she said softly, setting two cups on the table. "It's all part of the cycle, but it's still hard when..."

"When death wins," he finished as she paused, his expression looking as chiseled as stone.

"We have a new filly," she told him on a lighter note, pouring the coffee. "By Calaban out of Windraven's Fancy."

"Impressive bloodlines."

"Yes. She has magnificent legs. It's too early to tell, but I have a hunch she's champion material."

"Are you planning on racing her?"

"No. Rory and I are going for the Olympics."

Kyle lifted the cup in a toast. "Good luck."

Smiling at his skepticism, she removed bacon and eggs from the refrigerator and put a skillet on a burner. She decided to offer him breakfast. He accepted, and a few minutes later she placed it on the table.

He ate with appreciable gusto, and she was glad she'd thought of breakfast.

"Thanks," he said, wrapping his hands around the coffee cup when he finished. "I didn't come over for a meal, but I can't say I'm sorry I showed up without an invitation. Those were the best eggs I've had in a long spell."

"Mom made them this way for my dad. He said the same thing—"

Megan realized she'd entered forbidden territory when Kyle's face hardened. She held his gaze, refusing to apologize for mentioning her parents.

He stood and headed for the door. "I'll call you when the other gear gets here."

"All right."

She watched him leave, then got busy. Her first riding class was late getting started, one kid fell off his mount, fortunately without getting seriously hurt, and the cranky horse she was training tried to take a plug out of her leg. The day went downhill from there.

Evening shadows drew purple shades across the landscape when Megan entered the private study once more. She frowned at the desk. It, more than any piece of furniture in the house, reminded her of her grandfather—huge, forbidding and secretive. But for all his supposed fierceness, he had been a kind and gentle person to his granddaughters.

Setting her jaw, she sat down in the big leather chair and pushed the rolltop up. All the fascinating cubbyholes she'd wanted to explore as a child stared back at her like so many menacing eyes.

Starting at the first one on the top row to the left, she began working her way across. She smiled as she discarded ads on ranch equipment and old catalogs from seed companies and livestock stud farms.

She opened the stud brochure and studied the pictures of handsome bulls and read their statistics—weight, pedigree, the poundage of their offspring.

The lurking sadness hit her with a pang in the heart. She'd planned to have two perfect children, a boy and girl, by now. Naturally, she would also have had the perfect husband. As a family, they would work together on the ranch, their days filled with laughter and sunshine.

But none of that had come about. Her high-school sweetheart had gone off to the state university while she'd attended a community college and looked after her invalid grandfather, unable to leave him alone in the house after her father's death.

Sadly she reflected that when her steady had returned home the next summer, they'd found they had nothing to talk about. Their dreams had gone separate ways.

Dreams. A shudder rolled over her as she recalled the dreams that had haunted her all week. The old nightmares from her childhood had returned full force.

In them, there was always the soft, desolate sound of a woman crying. It broke her heart to even think about that soft, hopeless sobbing. No wonder the child had cried, too.

She closed her eyes and made herself listen. Like the dawn breaking, it came to her that the woman was her mother, something she had known but refused to acknowledge.

And that explained why the child, whom she knew to be herself, was so afraid. It was scary for a child to hear her mother cry. Mothers were supposed to make things better.

Megan pressed a hand to her aching chest and tried to recall the scene. Why had her mother been crying as if her heart were breaking? Why had it frightened her young self so much? Had her parents had a quarrel?

For a long minute she willed herself to remember,

but no further insights came to her. Sighing, she gave up and returned to her task.

She threw all the old stuff away—ads, catalogs, Christmas cards from presidents of companies and senators, letters from people she didn't know. Her grandfather had once figured prominently in political circles. He'd wanted his son to run for office....

"If you'd married the girl I told you to, you could have been governor by now. But no, you threw your future away on some little nobody. Think with your head, boy, not with—"

"To hell with that! And leave my wife out of it. I don't want to be governor. That's your dream, not mine."

"I never thought a son of mine would be a fool for some little floozy in skirts."

"Don't ever speak of my wife like that again!"

Megan brought her hands down to rest on the arms of the chair. She'd covered her ears instinctively as the hateful words drummed through her. She knew the scene had been real and that, as a child, she'd tried to block the ugly words by clapping her hands over her ears. She was positive she had listened to her grandfather and father quarrel, using those very words.

She exhaled shakily. No wonder the child hadn't wanted to hear. The mood had been ugly and hurting, the argument too harsh for a child to understand anything but the hatred in it.

Forcing her emotions at bay, she continued with the task at hand. She looked through every cubbyhole, all twenty-eight of them. Some were empty; she made sure by running her hand all the way to the back and checking carefully. Some contained rubber bands and paper clips, others pencils and pens or scribbled notes to pick up fertilizer or other ranch needs.

The last one held a surprise. Her grandfather had saved notes from her grandmother, written before they were married, one wishing him a happy birthday and telling of her adventures in Europe while on a tour for young ladies with the academy she'd attended.

Finishing school. It seemed a funny notion to Megan, who'd tolerated school and lived for the summers when she was free to roam the land she loved.

Her memories of her grandmother, who'd died when she was a three-year-old, were from stories her mother had told her of the woman's gentleness of spirit and kindness to the unexpected daughter-in-law her son had brought home when he graduated from college.

She finished reading the old postcard, then gasped. It wasn't from *her* grandmother; it was from Kyle's!

The old-fashioned scrolled signature at the bottom was that of Mary Dee Sloan. Her grandfather had saved it all these years, the last card from his fiancée before she'd returned to Wyoming and to him…and the wedding that had never taken place.

Pity for her grandfather rose in her. He'd never forgotten Mary Dee, his first love.

She wondered if her grandmother had known and

realized she must have. The gentle Rose had also been a resident of Wind River. She would have known of the engagement, of Mary's flight only days before the ceremony. Knowing she was the second choice, that she would never come first in his heart, she'd still accepted Patrick Windom. She must have loved him very much.

The desolate sadness overcame Megan as she sat there lost in the past. It had all happened a long time ago, yet it still affected their lives—

Hearing a clatter against the windows, she looked up, startled. Rain hit the glass with driving force. Pushing back from the desk, she rose and stood by the window, watching the storm sweep down from the western peak.

Weather was the bane of a rancher's existence. The rain was needed, but it was bad for the hay drying in the field. It rarely fell in July and August when wildfires raged out of control over much of the West and rain was desperately needed to cool and wash the dry land.

Restless, she checked the time. Almost ten.

After turning out the light, she walked down the dark hallway to the kitchen. Across the lake, she could see the lights of the Herriot house.

She'd never been inside, but she'd heard descriptions. Mrs. Herriot had been an interior decorator before her marriage. She'd had the place modernized, so Megan had heard. Kyle had his own wing in the rambling structure.

A tremor rushed along her nerves. He was alone

in his house as she was alone in hers. East and west, and never the twain shall meet. Enemies. And yet, she somehow wished she could go to him and find comfort in his arms. It was the strangest thing, this longing....

Kyle watched the rain sweep across the lake in sheets of gray. The storm had started last night and settled into a steady ground-soaker with the dawn.

He'd gone over the ranch books with the foreman of the three-thousand-acre spread that morning. The contractor who was to cut their hay wouldn't be able to work today, and the foreman was worried about having enough feed for the winter if they lost this cutting. The rain hadn't come at the right time for maximal growth, which would also affect the size of the sugar beet crop, one of their main income producers.

Weather was a rancher's life...and about as predictable as a woman's moods.

With a cynical snort, he refilled his coffee cup and updated the accounts on the computer. The family holdings included five buildings in town, which rented offices and store space to various businesses. One needed a new roof, which he had to have done before winter. Another was complaining about the rent and wanted it lowered. He had to make a decision about that.

None of this seemed of major importance this morning. His mind kept drifting into forbidden territory. Pictures of his neighbor, dressed only in a sexy swimsuit and high-heeled boots, formed in his mental vision. The swimsuit had been reality; the boots had been added in his dreams.

The ringing of the doorbell interrupted his musing. Going to the door, he half expected to find her there, demanding to know what he was doing about the sailboat.

A kid from the bakery in town grinned at him. "I'm supposed to sing *Happy Birthday,*" he announced.

Kyle grimaced. "Do you have to?"

"Nah. Here's your cake. Sign here."

Kyle signed the delivery slip and took the package.

"Have a happy birthday," the kid said on his way back to his car.

"Yeah, thanks." Kyle read the card on the box.

His mother had ordered his favorite, German chocolate cake, before leaving on her trip. Pleased, he went to the kitchen, removed the two candles shaped like numerals, and cut a large slice. While he ate, he contemplated the significance of the day.

Twenty-seven. He felt older.

He knew Megan had turned twenty-six in May. Funny, to know Megan's age and birth month when they had rarely spoken to each other. It was just that he recalled odd bits and pieces about her.

Because of her connection to his father's death?

A sharp spike of anger darted through him. The Windoms were known for their tempers. They had been among the earliest settlers in this valley. Their land had once amounted to over twenty thousand acres. At five thousand, it was still substantial and consisted of some of the best pastures and cropland in the vicinity. His grandfather always said Patrick Windom thought he was lord of all he surveyed.

His grandmother, once engaged to the man, had kept curiously silent on the subject. But then, their lives, the Windoms' and the Herriots', had been lived separately, each on his or her own side of the lake.

The ringing of the telephone jarred his morbid thoughts. He downed the last bite of cake with a swig of coffee before answering. "Herriot."

"Kyle, this is Shannon. Happy birthday."

"Hi. Thanks."

"You're to come over tonight for a birthday dinner. No arguments. I promised your mother before you left that I'd see to it."

"Mm, sounds as if you and my mom are in cahoots. Does this mean that in the future, I'll have to watch out for you two?"

"Maybe," was all she'd admit, then she laughed, too. "I confess. We did consult about it. She mentioned at the wedding that she hated it that you would be alone on your birthday, so, being the wonderful neighbor that I am, I volunteered Rory to grill steaks for the occasion. Your mom felt much better about leaving after that, and I knew you'd want her to have a good time."

He had to laugh at her airy explanation. "Okay, what time do you want me?"

"Is seven okay?"

"Sure. Don't bother with a cake. Mom ordered

one from the bakery, which was just delivered. I'll bring it over."

"Great. See you at seven."

She hung up before he could ask if any other members of her family, namely Megan, would be present. He cursed and forced himself back to the computer. It was late afternoon before he finished bringing all the accounts up to date.

A weak sun peeked out from the clouds when he went outside to check his prize mare. She greeted him with a whuffle of eagerness and stuck her nose against his chest, waiting for a rub.

He scratched her ears and under her mane, liking the smooth, warm hide under his fingers. "Hey, girl," he murmured. "Miss your baby, do you? Next year we'll do better. No more breech births, though."

For the oddest moment, he became lost in thoughts of births and babies and family. His mother had lost two children at birth and hadn't been able to have more.

He'd always wanted brothers and sisters. Being the only kid on a ranch had been lonely in some ways. He'd like a couple of kids, maybe three or four, but definitely more than one. He felt the emptiness in his life and wondered why he was thinking along these lines.

The foreman and his son, who handled the livestock, were busy at their chores. Kyle helped with the horses and the prize cow ponies the ranch was known for. He found the work relaxing after dealing with cash balances and numbers all day. Shortly before seven, he showered, dressed and retrieved the cake box from the kitchen. He fetched a bottle of merlot and headed for his friend's house.

"Yo, neighbor," Rory greeted him when he stepped out of the pickup. "Come on out back. I've got the charcoal going."

He went to the back porch of the cottage where Rory and his bride lived while the larger house next door, which had belonged to Rory before the wedding, was being remodeled as their family home. He wondered if that meant there would be children soon.

"The girls are in the kitchen," Rory informed him, "in case you want to say hello and leave your stuff. That wine looks good. A merlot? Shannon's favorite."

"Good." Kyle's heart picked up its beat as he entered the kitchen.

From the back, the two women looked very similar with slender but shapely builds, both dressed in jeans and long-sleeved shirts. Shannon's hair was darker than Megan's, but both women had enough auburn to be considered redheads.

"Kyle, you're here," Shannon greeted him, coming forward to give him a hug.

He opened his arms and leaned down to return the warm welcome. "Where shall I put these?" he asked.

"Do you mind if we cool the wine a little?"

"Not at all. I like it that way, too."

"Good. Megan, find the wine cooler, will you—that silver bucket Rory's office staff gave us for a wedding present—and fill it with ice? It's in one of the cabinets on the other side of the stove. Is this the promised cake?'' she asked Kyle.

''Right.''

Shannon peered at the cake box. She was legally blind due to having tunnel vision, but with her glasses on, she could read and seemed to do okay. ''Yum, German chocolate.''

''Right again.''

He placed the box on the counter and turned to Megan. ''Hello. How's it going?''

''Hi. Fine.''

She didn't look at him as she busied herself looking in cabinets until she found the bucket. Kyle put the bottle of wine in the bucket and held it in place while she dropped ice cubes in.

Her hands brushed his twice as she worked. An electric tingle shot up his arm each time. Meeting her eyes, he knew she felt it, too. Without pausing to consider the action, he reached up and ran a fingertip along her bottom lip.

Obviously flustered, she backed away. ''I need to finish the salad.''

She set the cooler aside, out of the way of marinating steaks and the makings of a salad. The familiar heaviness settled low in his body, causing an ache he didn't want or need. Neither the time nor the woman was right.

The silence stretched between them. He couldn't think of a thing to say.

Luckily Shannon had no such problem. ''How's

the mare? Rory said she had a tough birth and you lost the colt.''

Rory was the local vet as well as an expert horse breeder. He and Megan were working on a program to produce champion show-jumping stock.

Kyle ignored something akin to jealousy toward his old friend as he answered. ''She's recovering okay. I think she misses the baby. She keeps calling the way mothers do when separated from their young.''

''Poor thing,'' Shannon murmured.

He glanced at Megan. A look of intense sadness crossed her face, then, catching his gaze, she gave him a bland stare and went back to making the salad.

Shannon poked a fork through the potatoes baking in the oven. ''Almost done,'' she said. ''Would you mind taking the steaks out?'' she asked him.

''No problem.''

He would be glad to leave the icy atmosphere. Tension radiated from Megan like radio waves off an antenna. He didn't like the vibes he was getting from her. She would rather he hadn't come. Well, it was only for one night. She could grin and bear it the same as him. He carried the steaks out to their host.

Megan finished the salad while Shannon set the old-fashioned round table in the kitchen. ''How's your dream house coming along?''

''Slowly. The floor men finally showed up. The sanding is done and the first coat of polyurethane is down. Can you believe there were three coats of paint over oak flooring?''

''People do strange things.''

Shannon peered at the table. ''Did I forget anything?''

''Nope. Shall I put the rolls in the oven?''

''No. Take them out to the men. Rory can warm them on the grill.''

Well, she'd asked, Megan reminded herself as she went out the door. She avoided looking at her enemy as she handed over the basket of sourdough rolls.

When everything was ready, the four of them gathered around the family-style table. Shannon passed the platters around. ''Megan rescued this table from the attic over the storage shed,'' she told the men. ''It was pretty beat up, but she stripped the old varnish, then we sanded until our arms nearly dropped off. Didn't it turn out nice?''

''Yes,'' Kyle said. ''My mother likes to find treasurers, as she calls them, in people's barns and sheds, only she doesn't redo them.''

''That's the latest trend in decorating, having old things about. It's called shabby chic,'' Megan said.

''There's a psychological reason behind that,'' Shannon informed them. ''It makes people feel good to have old, used items in the house. It's a link to the past, one might say.''

''But buying an old pie safe or dresser at an antique store has nothing to do with the purchaser's past.''

''True,'' Shannon agreed with her cousin, ''but

that isn't the point, or not the whole of it. It's the sense of connection that counts, as if the past were somehow present in the item. I think people need a feeling of permanence in their lives. Families are so mobile and scattered nowadays."

"Which seems odd, especially since we're all living so much longer," Kyle said. "You'd think whole families would be together in multi-generation households again."

A scene from the past came to Megan—her grandfather shouting at her mother, her father looking grim. "Sometimes that doesn't work out. Sometimes it makes life hard...."

She paused as three pairs of eyes looked at her, Shannon's and Rory's sympathetic, Kyle's speculative, as if he suspected mayhem in the Windom home.

"But," she continued, "it's probably always been a difficult adjustment, having several generations to accommodate in a single household."

"Yes, but people manage," Shannon added on a lighter note. "Darling, would you pour the wine? I totally forgot about it."

After Rory served the merlot, the talk drifted to the happenings in the valley and surrounding area, then to the common problems of ranching. Shortly before ten, Megan helped Shannon serve dessert. When they finished, she stood.

"Tomorrow comes early, I'm afraid. I'd better head home. Thanks for a lovely evening." She hugged the newlyweds, said good-night to Kyle and left.

He followed her out the door, going to his truck while she went to the station wagon. When she turned the key, something gave a click, but the engine didn't start. After several tries, Kyle came over.

"Sounds as if your battery is dead."

She nodded.

"I'll give you a jump-start." He got cables out of his vehicle and attached them to hers. In a minute the engine was purring softly.

Rory, observing from the back porch, waved them off when they left. Megan tensed when Kyle turned left and followed her to her house instead of going to his own on the far side of the lake. When she stopped in the driveway, he did, too. He rolled down his window when she got out.

"I thought I'd make sure you got home okay."

"Thanks."

She stood there, aware of moonlight all around them. The wind whispered through the cottonwoods, flipping the leaves over and exposing their silvery lining. A copse of aspens shimmered eerily in black and silver, like ladies dancing at a midnight ball, their dresses sparkling from the light of a million stars.

The soft snick of a lock warned her a second before Kyle stepped out of the truck.

Her heart beat very fast.

Without a word, he enfolded her in his arms, his mouth descending, a hungry predator searching for its prey. And without a protest, she lifted her mouth to his, eager for his kiss, even as warnings resounded throughout her.

He was the danger she welcomed…had longed for.

His hands at her waist guided her back a step, then he lifted her so that she sat on the seat of the pickup. He guided her knees to each side of his hips as he stepped closer so that they touched intimately.

Heat spread from that place of joining, radiating outward, warming the night air around them. She laid her hands against his chest and felt his heart beating.

"This is so…"

"Yes," he agreed, sweeping across her face and biting gently along her neck to her throat.

When he ran his tongue into the hollow there, she gasped and raised her hands to his shoulders, needing to hold on.

"Why?" she asked.

"It just is. Like air. Like breathing." He raised his head. "I need to see you, touch you."

The moment balanced on a silver thread. The warning inside her became urgent. She ignored it and nodded.

When he reached for her buttons, she did the same, unfastening one for one until they were both finished.

Then his lips were on her, burning, feeding the flames inside until the last clamors of sense were like ashes blowing through her hazy mind.

"It's torture," he murmured. "The need…it haunts my nights…my every moment."

"I know." She eagerly sought his warmth, resentful when she touched cotton instead of flesh. She tugged at the T-shirt until it was free of his jeans and her hands could skim over his smooth flesh. "You're warm, so warm."

"So are you. Like fire. You burn me up."

His hands cupped her breasts, making her start as fresh swirls of passion spread through her.

"Easy," he whispered.

"Not easy," she protested. "Nothing is ever easy."

"It could be. Making love to you would be the easiest thing I ever did."

Reaching behind her, he unclipped her bra, then it and her shirt slid away. His hands were there to warm her at once, caressing her back down to her jeans, up to her nape.

"You make me feel so…wanted," she said as he bent to her breasts, tonguing her nipple until it was one hard aching point, then going to the other.

"I do want you. I can't hide it," he added, anger mixed with resignation. "It doesn't make sense, but it's there."

She caught his face between her hands and planted little skimming kisses all over it. He leaned into her, then surprised her as he moved against her, his rigid length pressing into her with greater intimacy. She was ready for him, she realized.

It seemed like a miracle, this heat, this passion. "How could I have lived this long without knowing this?"

"We weren't ready."

"But...we are...now?" Talking, even breathing, was almost more than she could manage at this moment.

"Yes. I don't know. Maybe." His tone was low, husky, driven by needs he didn't want to acknowledge, but couldn't ignore.

What happened to him when she was around? Why her? Why now? It was a mystery, part of the larger one he was trying to solve—the involvement of his father with her mother. Danger swirled around him like a fatal cloud of poison.

But she didn't feel like poison; she felt like honey, sweet and tempting.

He touched her breasts and felt the flames inside leap, burning into that sensitive part of him that suddenly ached for things he couldn't name.

She was part of the longing...this woman in his arms...this lovely enemy who made him forget the past and ignore the future. When she moaned slightly, her hands roaming over his torso, he was lost to reason. Whatever was between them, it affected her as well as him.

Pushing against her, he felt a tremor run through her slender frame. He shuddered as desire flamed higher, driven by their mutual need.

"Need you," he heard himself say, a confession. "It's hell, this wanting."

"Yes. I know," she answered feverishly. She wondered why she hadn't exploded by now as a new, wild force built within, obscuring the moonlight, adding to the haziness that made clear thinking impossible. "It's strange. To find this now, with you."

"The enemy," he finished for her.

He became very still. So did she. Only the pounding of their hearts, still pulsing with needs unmet, reminded her of the tumult between them. She felt his anger before he spoke.

"The other time I kissed you, I vowed it wouldn't happen again." He laid a hand over her heart. "It isn't all pretense. You can't fake everything."

"What pretense? Fake what?" she asked in confusion.

"Your response. Do you intend to use my passion for you to keep me away from the truth?"

He stepped away, and cold rushed in to fill the space between them. She missed the closeness. His eyes, so dark in the moonlight, were as cold as the ice pack that gleamed on the peaks around them.

"No," she said slowly, sadly. Then, with icy detachment from the madness of passion, she repeated the denial. "No. I want the truth as much as you. More. Because you blame my mother, and I know she was innocent."

His laughter was quick, harsh. "Like you?" he questioned, catching her chin and running his thumb over her lip. "An innocent? I think not. Is your passion real…or calculated?"

She pushed his hand away, hurt by the suspicion in his voice. "Let me know when you figure it out," she suggested as she grabbed her clothing. Using it as a shield, she forced herself to walk with dignity up the sidewalk to the dark mansion that waited for her. The cold of the night chilled her flesh and her heart.

"I will," he promised softly.

From the shadows beside the creek, she heard the swift flutter of wings, then the startled squeak of a small creature who'd foolishly ventured into the night.

Inside the lonely mansion, she buried her face in the crumpled shirt and felt the most desolate sense of isolation she'd ever known.

Chapter Six

Today is the third Saturday of June, early morning. My wedding day! I didn't think it would ever arrive!

Megan read the entry in the neat handwriting belonging to her grandmother. It had been fifty years since the bride had penned those words. Such a long time.

Today was also the third Saturday in June. Megan stared absently at the calendar, then focused once more on her tasks. She was going through the drawers of the massive oak desk, intent on getting the chore done. She'd found the drawers locked on one side of the desk. Fortunately, she had her grandfather's set of keys.

As a child, she'd found the keys fascinating. Her grandfather had always carried them on a silver loop on his belt. The keys had made the patriarch seem powerful and mysterious, the keeper of the family treasures, and maybe its secrets, assuming there were any.

There had been no treasure, as she'd found when he'd had the stroke. Kate, with her usual quiet efficiency, had put together a plan to keep the ranch intact so that the three cousins had kept their legacy.

Were there family secrets? Maybe her grandmother's journals would tell her. Placing them back in the drawer for later reading, she continued through the records of the past, learning of disastrous drops in beef prices, the loss of a sugar beet crop to a late freeze, all the myriad things that beset those who worked with nature.

At one, she stopped and decided to take a ride to clear the cobwebs from her brain. She packed a lunch and, on impulse, selected the first journal—the bride's journal, she named it—before heading for the stable.

''Be a gentleman today,'' she told the cranky gelding, who actually seemed glad to see her—until she tried to mount, then he swung around, teeth bared.

''No teeth,'' she warned.

Naturally he didn't heed her words. He had to learn she meant business. She gave him a squirt of citronella, a new tactic accomplished by adapting the old joke of a plastic flower attached to a water bottle. She'd pinned the end of the spray tube to her jeans at knee level.

He snorted and sneezed and looked totally surprised.

Laughing softly, Megan swung into the saddle and clicked her tongue. He obeyed immediately.

"Good boy," she said. "You learn fast."

She rode through the broad sloping pasture to the far fence. Guiding the gelding to the gate, she opened and closed it without a hitch. From there she rode toward the white gazebo down by the lake.

As soon as she started to dismount, the gelding swung around again. She gave him another squirt, saying firmly, "No teeth."

He tossed his head and snorted as before, then rolled a suspicious eye in her direction.

"Yeah, I've got lots of tricks up my sleeve," she told him, tying the reins to the railing of the gazebo and loosening the saddle.

The gelding fell on the fresh green grass next to the lake like a miser finding gold.

She took her lunch and the journal to the benches built around the sides of the gazebo. Rose's Folly, the family had called it, after her grandmother who'd wanted it built. Her own middle name, Rose, was for the grandmother she couldn't recall from the mists of her childhood.

While munching on a sandwich, she opened the journal and reread the opening line. Why did the journal begin with her wedding day rather than continuing from her youth? Surely she'd had a diary. Was the new journal to commemorate her new life as the Windom bride?

Probably. Her grandmother had had a sense of the dramatic as well as a sentimental streak.

She continued reading of the couple's first days. A honeymoon in New York. Interesting. She tried to imagine her grandfather at the fancy hotel, the theater, the dinner parties described by Rose. Megan realized her grandmother had been part of an influential circle.

By the end of the journal, Rose had miscarried and was obviously depressed about it. She wanted a child very much. A single-line entry ten months into the marriage startled Megan. She learned that her grandfather's former fiancée, Mary Dee, now married to Sonny Herriot, was expecting.

The hair stood up on Megan's neck at this observation on the part of her grandmother. For a moment, she wondered if that child, who became the man who had died with her mother on the lake fifteen years ago, could have been her grandfather's child. But no. The timing was off. Mary Dee and Sonny would have been married thirteen months by then.

She read on. The last entry in the journal mentioned the birth of Mary's son…and that Rose was expecting a child, too. Her own father, Sean Windom, had been born six months after the Herriot heir.

Her mind lost in the past, Megan closed the journal. She drank the last of the iced tea she'd brought while she mused on the lives of her ancestors. But for a quirk of fate, Mary Dee would have been her grandmother, instead of Kyle's. What had driven the woman from Grandfather's side?

The rumble of thunder brought her attention to the soaring peaks surrounding her.

A summer thunderstorm. The kind that often brought little rain, but much lightning, sparking the forest fires that could rage out of control for weeks, destroying trees, pastures, homes and lives.

She packed up, tightened the girth and grabbed the horse's reins. The gelding swung his head around. She waited, one foot in the stirrup.

He paused, evidently thinking things over, then dipped his head closer to her leg. She tensed her fingers on the pump bulb at her waist.

The gelding lunged. She squeezed three times in succession. Citronella filled the air. She and the horse both sneezed. He shook his head from side to side and snorted indignantly.

Laughing, she mounted while he was thus occupied, then tightened her knees, turning him toward home.

Hearing a noise behind her, she twisted in the saddle and glanced over the lake. Kyle glided up to the island of granite and tossed the anchor overboard. She watched as he donned a wet suit and scuba gear, then disappeared over the side of the motorboat.

Fury washed over her. He wasn't keeping his end of the bargain by including her in his plans. It came to her that he'd never intended to. He wanted to bring the sailboat up and discover whatever it would disclose all by himself.

Two could play at that game.

She wheeled around and leaned forward. ''Get up, you mangy critter,'' she ordered the gelding, who leaped to do her bidding. She smiled grimly. One recalcitrant male under control. Now for the other one....

Megan heard the roar of the engine long before the boat reached the dock at her place.

''Hi, you're just in time for dinner,'' she called out to her guest as he stalked up the yard to the patio.

''You rented the compressor,'' he said in a snarl of ill-temper.

''So I did. How clever of you to discover it.''

His dark brows drew together. His eyes narrowed dangerously. He looked ready to explode.

Time for Act Two.

She'd showered and dressed carefully before starting dinner. Her golden earrings with a long fall of freshwater pearls were deliciously feminine brushing against her neck as she looked up at her enemy. She'd put on perfume and makeup. Her outfit, black slacks and matching jacket over a beige shell, was charmingly simple. Black high-heeled sandals made her feel wickedly sexy.

She turned fully toward Kyle, her smile carefully in place, a reckless challenge blazing within.

His chest lifted as he inhaled sharply, his eyes taking in every inch of her appearance. Fire suddenly glowed in the smoky depths, turning them into molten silver.

"What are you going to do with it?" he demanded.

She was all innocence. "Why, bring up the sailboat. Isn't that what we agreed we were going to do?"

He looked like a man who wanted nothing so much as to tackle her on the spot and make her cry uncle and hand over the equipment so he could get on with the job.

She wouldn't.

He muttered an expletive.

"Such language and from a guest. How do you like your hamburger? I usually cook mine well done."

He grabbed her shoulders as if he would give her a good shaking. She leveled a warning glare at him.

An eternity ticked past, numbered by the beats of her heart as she held her ground.

His grip eased, then fell away.

"The sailboat is mine," he told her. "It belonged to my father. It'll belong to me."

"The laws of salvage says it belongs to whoever brings it up. That's *us,* as in we'll own it jointly. That's why the compressor rental is in my name."

"So you're staking your claim."

"That's right. I also told the store owner, the sheriff and a couple of ranchers who happened to be present exactly what we were doing."

"By now the whole county knows."

"Probably. You know," she said conversationally, "the insurance company could try to make a claim.

It paid off on the policy, so it'll try to recoup the loss.''

''To hell with that.''

''There were over a hundred insurance claims lodged when the *Titanic* was found.''

''What happened?''

''I understand they were settled out of court for a percentage of the estimated value.''

He cursed again.

She shrugged. Turning her back on him, she went to the grill to flip the hamburgers and vegetables over. ''There're chips and dip on the table, beer and wine in the cooler. Help yourself.''

''The perfect hostess,'' he muttered, but he selected a beer, poured her a glass of wine and brought it over. ''Here's to success,'' he said sardonically.

''Yes—ours,'' she agreed, lifting her glass. They clinked bottle to glass, then drank, each watching the other, enemies in an age-old struggle for control.

The sizzle of meat reminded her of her duties. She toasted the buns, then took up the food on a huge Mexican platter of bold colors and exotic birds. She and her parents had visited the country once, and her mother had bought a set of matching serving pieces.

Which had made her grandfather furious when he'd seen the souvenirs. She suddenly remembered his unkind words to her mother about her extravagance.

Did you think you'd married into a gold mine when you got my son?

She wished her grandfather had been different. Kinder. Gentler. More understanding.

However, she now knew the ranch had been in financial trouble at the time. Rose's inheritance, brought into the marriage, had staved off bankruptcy once, but wasn't enough to carry the place forever.

"My grandfather probably married my grandmother for her money," she said, combining her knowledge with the day's revelations in the journal. "I just realized it. And he accused my mother of being a fortune hunter." This last was spoken rather indignantly.

Kyle ignored the colorful platter she placed on the table. "Did you remember something about them?"

"Not exactly. I was reading in Grandmother Rose's journal today, though. It started with her wedding day."

"Three months after my grandfather and grandmother married."

Megan was silent while she fixed her meal and began eating, her mind on the woman who was supposed to have been her grandmother rather than Kyle's. "Did you ever consider that your grandfather was the man who betrayed his best friend and married that friend's fiancée immediately after a quarrel, before they had a chance to make up?"

"I think she was damned lucky to get away from Patrick Windom," he said.

Megan mulled over the unfortunate triangle—quadrangle, if she included her grandmother—and wondered what the truth was. After thinking about that, she said, ''Bringing up the boat won't solve that mystery.''

''Which one is that?''

His question implied there were many where her family was concerned. She felt his distrust like the cold blade of a sharp knife. ''Why Mary Dee married another only days before her wedding. Did she regret the rash decision? Did she long for my grandfather during the years she was married to your grandfather? You have to wonder about it all.''

Kyle glared at her. ''My grandmother was very happy with her husband and her life. She made the right choice.''

''But he wasn't her first choice,'' she said, compelled to point out this obvious fact.

Kyle didn't answer. She pushed her plate aside after a couple more bites and sipped the wine.

The moon was half full, but on the wane. Each night its light would grow less until it was only a sliver of light in the night sky. Then it would brighten again.

Life was like that. Right now, hers was at one of the low points in its cycle, but it would change as all of life did, ebbing and flowing with the tides of fate and fortune.

Perhaps when she and Kyle were finished with their task, her heart would be at ease once more.

She glanced at him and felt her pulse quicken. Restless energy poured through her even though she'd been tired when she'd finished the ranch chores.

From the time she'd become involved with Kyle, perforce during the wedding plans and rehearsal, and afterward due to their search for answers to their mutual past, she'd experienced the magnetic pull of her enemy.

It tugged at her now, making her want fulfillment, urging her to throw caution to the wind, as the cliché went, and take what she wanted.

"Don't look at me that way," he warned suddenly, "unless you're issuing an invitation."

"I'm not," she quickly denied. "Not intentionally."

"Then I eagerly await the day your intentions correspond to your..."

She willed herself not to respond, no matter what damaging word he chose.

"...desires," he finished softly, derisively.

He had the power to hurt her. She didn't think he even realized how much. She wasn't sure herself. Through adamant self-control, she calmed the hot glaze of emotion that knotted her throat until she could speak once more.

"That'll never happen. I would never be so foolish as to trust a Herriot the way Mary Dee and my mother did."

"Which is why you rented the compressor," he concluded in cold amusement. "You're right. I planned on bringing the wreck up and not letting you know. I went to town to get the compressor this afternoon and found out my *partner* had already rented it."

The stark declaration shocked her. "You dare admit it?"

"Why not?" He shrugged. "Don't worry. I intended to let you know the truth when I found it."

She stared into the dark red wine left in her glass. She made herself speak very softly. "But would you twist the truth to suit your view of history?"

His hand jerked slightly as he formed a fist at his side, then deliberately relaxed it. He lifted the beer bottle. "To the real truth," he said mockingly and finished off the brew.

Lifting the glass to her lips, she drank the rich red wine. It tasted of grapes and oak tannin and bitterness. Her hand trembled slightly when she set the empty crystal container on the table.

Megan was expecting the phone call from Kyle the next day. Sure enough, the phone was ringing when she walked into the house shortly after the noon hour. She'd just returned from church. He must have been watching for her.

"Hello?" she answered, laying her Bible on the kitchen counter and kicking off her sandals.

"Are you ready to go out with the compressor?" he asked without bothering with a greeting.

"I'll need help getting it into the dory."

"It would bc easier to use my boat."

"Fine."

"I'll be over in ten minutes."

"I'll be ready," she said, as cool in tone as he was.

Hanging up, she picked up the Bible and sandals and headed for her room. She quickly changed to a bathing suit, then pulled on an old pair of sweats and sneakers. When Kyle arrived at the dock, she was already there.

"We'd better hurry," he said. "There's supposed to be a storm front coming in late this afternoon."

"The compressor is still in the wagon."

He nodded and followed her to the old station wagon that had served the ranch for fifteen years. "You got a couple of two-by-sixes?"

"In the shed, I think."

After finding a couple of boards, he placed them on the tailgate, then rolled the heavy compressor down the makeshift ramp. Rolling it along the lawn was more difficult. The wheels sank into the soft spots—inducing a couple of muffled expletives—more than once on the way to the dock.

"Hasn't Harry ever heard of new equipment?" Kyle asked when they got stuck for the third time.

"Is the newer stuff lighter than this?"

"More compact. These behemoths were replaced twenty years ago with a better design."

At the boat, he frowned as he looked her over. "You think Jess and his son are available to help heave this on board?"

"Maybe. What if we put the boards on the dock and the boat? Could we roll it across then?"

He brightened. "Good idea."

Megan had to scold herself as pleasure rolled over her at his offhand compliment. She went with him to get the two-by-sixes. In another few minutes, the deed was done.

"Okay, let's be off," he said impatiently.

"I haven't had lunch. Have you?"

"I brought sandwiches."

She turned toward the house. "I have some chips and fresh brownies Kate sent over. We can eat on the way," she added, seeing the impatience in his stance.

He nodded absently, his attention on the regulator and other devices on their equipment. She hurried back up the sloping lawn.

Fifteen minutes later, they were on their way. She found sandwiches and sodas in a cooler. He set their direction, then joined her in the quick meal.

At the granite island, he tied up, then glanced at her. "The wet suits arrived. We need to check you out in yours."

"Right. That's why I thought we needed the compressor. I saw you on the lake in a wet suit yesterday."

His expression tightened. "Where were you?"

"At the gazebo. I was working with one of the horses, training him to be a gentleman."

He gave a snort of laughter. "You women are always trying to tame some poor male until you have him eating from your palm."

"Not tame, civilize," she corrected. "It's a thankless job, but somebody has to do it."

"Ouch!" he murmured, grabbing his chest and pretending to pull out a dart.

She had to laugh, although it felt odd to joke with the enemy. When he started to strip down, she sobered, once again aware of the tension between them—and the dangerous hunger that made her ache for his touch.

"Try these on," he ordered, removing a wet suit from a locker.

She crossed her arms, grabbed the end of her shirt and pulled it over her head. After slipping the pants off, she struggled into the black neoprene outfit. It was short in the arms and legs so that she had to leave the sleeves unzipped, but otherwise okay.

"There's a hood."

She caught the matching headgear and pulled it on. "I'm beginning to feel like a mummy."

He zipped the sleeves on his suit. "Okay, let's try the tanks." He held the equipment so she could slip her arms through the straps.

The weight felt awkward on her back. She studied the dangling straps.

"These go between your legs," Kyle explained, reaching under her to pull the straps between her thighs and hook them onto the ones that clipped around her waist.

A flush burned through her even though he was careful to keep his touch impersonal. He quickly checked the regulator and had her practice breathing through it. He told her how to clear her face mask in case she got water in it.

"Do we have to worry about the bends?" she asked.

''Not at these depths. It's the cold that's dangerous in these waters. It can affect your thinking. If you feel muddled at all, come to the surface and get out. Don't go back in until you're thoroughly warm.'' He frowned thoughtfully. ''I should have brought a container of hot, sweet tea. That's one of the best things to bring up your internal temperature and chase out the chill.''

''Next time, I'll remember.''

He flashed her a glance she couldn't read, then nodded. He handed her an underwater light and showed her where to turn it on. She clipped it into place around her head.

''Are we going to try to float the sailboat today?''

After a quick shake of his head, he slipped on his own set of tanks, checked the breathing apparatus, then told her they were ready for a test dive as he adjusted his light.

Her heart pounded as she grabbed the flippers and slipped over the side by falling backwards off the boat. Panic set in for a second, then she was back at the surface and holding on to the swim-out rail.

Inhaling carefully, she found she could breathe through the mouthpiece. Putting on the flippers, she held up her thumb, indicating she was ready.

Kyle grinned behind his mask. She realized he knew of the flash of panic. She relaxed and smiled back to let him know she was okay now.

He looked at his watch, clipped on a weight belt, handed one to her and helped her into it. She wasn't sure she liked being weighed down in water that was a hundred feet deep if she missed the shelf where the boat was. She could see herself sinking straight to the bottom, unable to get back to the surface.

When he flicked on his light, she did the same.

To her surprise, he took her hand and, indicating they were to dive, headed for the bottom. She felt much safer paddling along with him close beside her.

As they neared the boat, she forgot about depending on a tank of air to breathe and the cold that tried to take her breath away. Focusing on the wreck, she followed Kyle as he made a circle of the hull.

When he let go of her hand, she followed him as he dived deeper. She saw the hole in the side and experienced a swift stab of pain as she wondered if her mother had struggled, knowing she was drowning even though she was unconscious from the blow to the head.

Kyle explored the break in the hull thoroughly, then he motioned toward the deck. Going up, she held on to the railing and saw he'd already moved all the rocks except for the big boulder from the bow. He'd certainly been busy.

She explored the deck, then peered into the dark hatch. She could see the galley and beyond that, the narrow quarters that served as a bedroom.

A shadowy picture of a man and a woman locked in a romantic tryst in the forward compartment came to her. She shook her head, refusing to accept the notion of her mother with another man.

Kyle took her wrist and, pulling her from the opening, guided her to the bow. She saw a long pry bar on deck. When he picked it up, she swam in close and took up a position in front of him, her hands on the bar. She looked a question at him.

When he nodded, she helped him get the bar into position under the rock, then they both pushed.

The boulder tilted, but not enough to clear the opening in the broken railing. Without bracing herself, she couldn't put any more force on the pry bar.

Kyle touched her shoulder and shook his head. He pointed to another large rock, then to her and the bar. She nodded. Holding the bar in place, she waited while he manhandled the rock into position.

He guided the rock onto the bar and, bracing his feet against the railing, he pushed the rock down on the bar. The boulder tilted several more degrees, but still not enough.

She had an idea. Going to the boulder, she pushed on it, then pointed to the bar. He caught on. They exchanged places. While he pushed, she shoved. That way, they got the pry bar farther under the boulder, then he picked up the rock while she held their position.

She kicked and pushed at the same time he shoved the rock down. They both struggled with all their might. Suddenly the boulder slipped forward, then, rolling and tumbling, fell overboard and sank out of sight.

Beneath her, the wreck gave a shudder, then the bow started lifting at the same time the stern skittered along the sloping ledge, heading toward deeper water. She heard a low rumble within the granite rock slide that had formed the island.

Hands grabbed her from behind. Kyle grasped her buttocks, then shoved her upward. She went sailing toward the surface. Kicking as hard as she could, she swam away from the dangerously shifting wreck. Kyle, she saw, was right behind her.

They hit the surface together.

He stripped off his mask. "That was close."

"What happened?" she asked, removing the mouthpiece.

"The boat shifted without the weight of the boulder to hold the bow down. There was another rock slide."

"Where? On the boat?"

"Under it, I think. Stay here. I'll go down and check."

"I'll go with you."

Kyle took one look at her set jaw and nodded. "Stay close. We'll try not to disturb the boat. I don't want it to go to the bottom."

"Why don't we tie some ropes to it and anchor it to the granite slab?"

"That's a thought. Hold on."

He swam to his boat, climbed out on the swim-out platform and retrieved a length of rope.

They went down again and studied the wreck. It teetered on the rocky ledge, looking as if it would sink out of sight at the slightest disturbance. Megan's spirits dropped.

If it wasn't one problem, it was another.

Kyle tied the rope to a deck cleat, then found a jagged edge to secure a knot. He motioned her to follow him.

Together they pushed at the back of the boat and managed to move it sideways along the ledge. He tightened the rope to hold it in place, then pointed upward.

She wanted to explore some more. Pointing toward the hatch, she indicated she wanted to look inside.

His lips formed the word *no*. Taking her hand, he shoved off, his long legs kicking powerfully as he headed up. They arrived back at the granite slab in time to hear a mighty crack, then the long rumble of thunder overhead.

Glancing at his watch, he grimaced. ''We were down way too long,'' he told her. ''It's time to go in. The storm is coming up a lot faster than we thought.''

She felt strangely buoyant, both in body and spirit. ''We'd be safe under the water,'' she told him.

''Unless there was another rock slide,'' he said, his tone sardonic. ''Or lightning hit the water.''

''It won't.'' She was quite confident.

''Come on,'' he said gruffly. ''You need to warm up.''

''I feel fine.''

''Right. That's when you have to worry the most, when you feel the best. That's why diving is dangerous.''

''Oh.'' She didn't feel in any danger at all.

He tossed his flippers on the swim-out, then the

weight belt. After doing the same with her stuff, he unfastened her tanks and put them on the platform. "Out," he said.

To her annoyance, she was amazingly awkward as she climbed onto the handy deck behind the boat. He stepped up behind her, steadying her until she clambered into the boat, then he followed.

She found her hands would hardly grasp the zipper when she tried to get out of the suit. Before she succeeded, Kyle's hands were there helping. He got her out of the clinging neoprene first, then stripped himself.

"Put on your clothes," he ordered.

"They'll get wet."

He flashed her a scowl. "You need the warmth."

After stowing the gear in the bench compartment, he started the engine. With a quick scan of the sky, he headed across the lake.

The rain hit them before they'd gone half-way. Hail joined the rain. They were drenched in less than two minutes. The air temperature dropped as if someone had opened a freezer door.

Megan realized how cold she was when her teeth started chattering. Huddled on the bench, making herself as small as possible, she shivered uncontrollably. Putting her jeans and shirt on over her bathing suit sounded like a good idea.

"Come here," Kyle said. He indicated the seat beside him and held out his arm for her to sit close.

She shook her head and struggled into her clothes. All at once, she felt tired and miserable and very,

very sad. The past weighed heavily on her spirits. "I wish my mother hadn't gone on that boat."

His face hardened, but he said nothing.

"Where are we going?" she asked after another minute of silence had passed, raising her voice above the clatter of rain and hail and wind.

"To my house to get warm. There's a hot tub."

A fresh wave of shivers rushed over her.

Chapter Seven

"Through here."

Megan followed Kyle into his house. The hallway floor was marble squares in a creamy shade of beige. The walls were papered in pale roses and green vines on a beige background that reminded her of antique paper. With the soft color and white wood trim, grapevine wreaths and dried flower arrangements, the decor was lovely, polite and refined.

Her own home was plain by comparison, with mostly white walls, massive furniture upholstered in leather and oak floors definitely showing their years. Only the kitchen, bathrooms and her parents' quarters had been updated in the last fifty years.

At the end of the hall, Kyle led her through double French doors that opened onto a screened patio. He folded back the cover, then flipped on the jets of a hot tub.

"Strip," he said.

Megan stared as he slipped out of his jeans and shirt. When he looked her way, she unfolded her arms and peeled down to her bathing suit. She couldn't control the trembling either inside or outside her body.

"Come."

She watched as he stepped into the steaming, bubbling water, then held a hand out for her. She hesitated, sure she shouldn't do this, but unable to refuse. Her instincts screamed *danger,* but her mind was curiously blank.

"Come," he said again, a note of impatience in the word as he waited for her.

She laid her hand in his and stepped into the froth of bubbles. A hidden bench provided a seat. Kyle joined her, sitting on the opposite side.

"I'm tingling," she told him, holding one hand out of the steaming water. "My hands and feet hurt, a sort of stinging sensation. Isn't that odd?"

"It's the heat after the intense cold."

"Oh."

His eyes were filled with thoughts she couldn't read—irony, perhaps; hunger, definitely—as he observed her. "Your lips are turning from blue to white. That's an improvement."

"Thanks. That bolsters my self-confidence at least three notches." She smiled and laid her head back, finding a neck rest molded into the tub.

His chuckle warmed her insides the way the water warmed the rest of her.

After a bit, the tingling subsided and was replaced by lethargy. She slipped into a doze, then abruptly awoke as her chin dipped below water level. Her feet brushed against Kyle's leg as they floated upward.

"Sorry," she murmured.

"That's okay."

He caught her ankles and tucked her toes under his thigh so that she didn't have to concentrate on keeping her feet under control. She wished they could stay there forever. She wished for a future instead of a past she couldn't recall. She wished that life could be different, but she couldn't define how....

Kyle tried to ignore the electricity that started at the place her toes touched his thigh and ran up his leg and into his groin. It was impossible. He was as aware of her as he was of sunlight.

She was a beautiful woman, this enemy of his.

He touched her foot, then lifted it into his lap and gently massaged her toes. Her skin was warm now. When she'd brushed against his thigh, her foot had been cold.

Anger pulsed through him. At himself. Forgetting her smaller body mass, he'd let her stay too long in the icy water in a wet suit that was too small. He should have been more careful with her.

She sighed and rolled her head to one side.

He brought her other foot into his lap and massaged the back of her heel, then her toes until he felt the tension ease completely. Moving upward, he rubbed the slender calves and used his thumbs to deep-massage the muscles, then the tendons behind her knees.

A low moan of pleasure-pain came from her.

He smiled, knowing exactly how she felt, and rubbed from her ankles to her knees. After a second's hesitation, he slid his hands over her thighs. She tensed slightly before relaxing again.

When her muscles, as strong and smooth as a trained athlete's, shifted under his touch, his response went from a mild stirring to demanding need.

Her eyes opened and met his.

He was suddenly aware of dark, mysterious depths that he wanted to explore and of a desire to be done with restraint and take what they both wanted.

Shaking his head at the wayward thought, he tucked her toes under his thigh again and tried to think of the sunken sailboat and the mystery surrounding it. He considered the facts that made this woman his enemy.

Nothing worked.

"I want you," he said, his voice surprising him. In spite of the bubbling water, the world around them seemed eerily quiet, as if it waited with bated breath to see what would happen next.

She voiced his thoughts. "It's difficult, isn't it…to feel this way about one's enemy?"

"Yes."

He couldn't help the huskiness of his voice or force his hand to move from where it had settled lightly on her knee, nor force his gaze away from her lips, which were rosy and moist from the steam.

Megan suppressed a gasp as his thumb brushed over her skin. She stared into his eyes as one in a daze. The world receded until there was only this moment, this space.

And a man and a woman who shouldn't have been there.

"Your mouth tears me apart," he told her, staring at her lips. "It makes me forget common sense."

She pressed her lips together to keep from urging him to do just that.

"I remember the taste of it, the feel. I wake and know I've been dreaming of kissing you."

"I've done that, too," she admitted.

"Do you dream of what happens after that?"

Her breath came out shaky. "Yes."

He moved closer, so close his thigh pressed against her bottom and his torso touched hers. With one hand, he guided her legs so that they rested across his lap, then draped his arm over her knees, his hand on her upper thigh.

A shiver, one of heat and delight, went through her.

"You're like quicksand," he continued. "A man could fall in and never get out, maybe never want to."

"I'm not like that." She spoke gravely, reprovingly.

His smile was quick, sardonic. "Maybe, but you

could lure a man into danger. One kiss and I'd forget everything but the hunger. I feel it now."

Desperation washed through her. "So do I," she whispered. "It hurts."

"Yes." His gaze softened. He lifted a hand and ran one finger over her lips. "The longing is the worst. At night. When I can't sleep."

"There are reasons for denying it."

He nodded. "Would you deny me if I were to kiss you?"

Rubbing lightly back and forth with just the one finger, he made her lips burn. She took his finger between her teeth to stop the tormenting action.

He sucked in a sharp breath when she ran her tongue over his fingertip. His eyes burned into hers.

"You make me want to take a bite out of you," he murmured, his eyelids dropping sexily over his intense gaze. "If I took your mouth, would I stop there? I don't think so. I'd want more. So would you."

Letting go, she nodded slightly. "Yes."

She laid her hand on his chest and turned toward him, knowing she was inviting the kiss...knowing and not caring.

"If I touched you here," he said and slid a hand down her throat, then trailed his fingers over her chest and into the valley between her breasts.

Her breath stopped.

"If I touched you here," he repeated as if to himself, "it would only be the beginning."

She forced air into her lungs and closed her eyes

against the fire in him, in her, and the insane longing to throw caution to the wind.

"It's confusing...." she began and stopped.

"The attraction between a man and woman?"

He smiled, his gaze flicking back to her eyes, devouring her and making her ache someplace deep inside. She nodded, troubled by it all.

"It's irresistible." He leaned toward her, his head dipping forward, his mouth close, so close. "It's hunger...and need, a longing from the soul."

For the briefest second, she saw pain in his eyes, then it was gone and there was only the hunger.

She couldn't be sure who moved first, or if they moved at all, but suddenly his lips were there, and she had only to raise her head, ever so little, for his lips to touch hers.

"It would be so easy," he murmured, his eyes narrowed, almost angry.

His hand closed over her breast, wringing a gasp of shock from her parted lips. But his touch was gentle. She could almost imagine that he cared.

"You could almost make me forget who you are when you respond like this," he murmured.

"Who am I?" she demanded. "Who am I to you?"

He gazed at her, his eyes dark and moody. "My beautiful enemy, that's who you are."

"As you are mine," she reminded him, angered by the words but not surprised by them.

"Yes."

He moved, and their lips almost touched. She could feel the kiss…the heat of his mouth…

The moment stretched between them, drawing taut, like a bowstring drawn to its fullest arc. She felt the pull deep inside, at the place she could be hurt, and acknowledged the danger of unleashing passion between them.

Time shifted, became still, then quivered like a young roe struck by a fatal arrow as the seconds slipped past. She took a breath and, summoning all her will, turned her head from the temptation of his mouth. She felt his breath against her cheek as he exhaled.

''You Windom women, you're like a drug. No wonder my father was sucked in,'' he whispered as if lost in his own thoughts and grievances.

''Perhaps my mother was sucked in, too, into a whirlpool that wasn't of her making,'' she suggested, keeping her tone cool and neutral as she moved away from him.

''Perhaps,'' Kyle conceded, but that was as far as he was willing to go. Until he learned the truth, there would always be questions between them. He climbed out, grabbed a couple of towels and tossed one to her.

When the phone rang, she visibly started. The muscles in his shoulders tensed. Neither moved. The phone announced its presence again, sounding angry and filled with self-importance in the silence.

As she climbed out of the hot tub, he grabbed the phone from the wall mount. ''Hello,'' he said gruffly.

His guest headed for the door.

"Wait," he ordered. "I'll take you home."

"Kyle?" his mother said. "Who are you talking to?"

He groaned silently. "Nobody." At Megan's glance, he smiled grimly. "Megan Windom," he said to his mother.

"She's at the house?" his mother demanded in disbelief.

"Yes." He couldn't think of a thing to add to that.

Megan paused in pulling on her wet sweatpants and shirt. She smiled wryly, her gaze daring him to explain further. He cast a grimace her way, then forced his eyes elsewhere to concentrate on what his mother was saying.

"You're not…surely you aren't seeing her."

The demand for reassurance was met with silence. Was he seeing Megan? Not in the usual sense, but they were partners in the salvage operation.

And there was the attraction thing.

"Hardly," he finally admitted. "She was caught out on the lake in a storm. I brought her here to warm up in the hot tub." Which sounded perfectly reasonable to him.

His mother gasped as if he'd announced plans to become a serial killer. He frowned and suppressed impatience. It had been a long time since he'd felt it necessary to explain himself to anyone, much less his mother.

Once they had talked about girls he had dated. With his father gone, his mother had taken on the

role of making sure he knew about the birds and bees and the consequences of letting hormones get out of hand. He regretted the flippant tone of his reply.

Glancing up, he noticed his troublesome neighbor was grinning. What had he said to shock his mother and amuse his enemy?

''I suppose you joined her,'' his mother said, her shocked disapproval coming through loud and clear. She sighed. ''It's none of my business. Just be careful. For your own sake.''

The implication of dire consequences in his dealings with Megan had him gritting his teeth against a retort. ''I'm always careful,'' he said on a light note. ''Are you having fun? Are the plays as good as advertised?''

They chatted a few minutes. He told her he'd got the birthday cake and that he'd spent the evening with Shannon and Rory and had a fabulous supper.

''Was the Windom girl there?''

''Yes.'' The curtness of his tone surprised him.

His mother seemed to understand the topic was off-limits. She talked briefly about New York and its attractions, then told him good-night. Megan raised one insolent eyebrow when he hung up.

''What?'' he growled.

''She suspects the worst. About us.''

He shrugged.

''Why didn't you tell her the truth?''

''About the salvage operation?'' He shook his head. ''She was hurt enough by the past. I see no need to bring it up.''

"What if we bring the boat up?" At his silence, she added, "It gets more complicated, doesn't it?"

"It wouldn't. If you'd stay out of it."

"No way. I have as much at stake here as you do."

"The truth, that's all I want."

"Me, too. With no other complications."

He laughed and heard the edge of bitterness in it. "Those are already here." He deliberately looked her over, then wished he hadn't. Her damp clothing clung to her slender body. She was shivering again. He wanted to be the one who warmed her up...all the way through.

"Come on," he said. "I'll take you home."

He grabbed a jacket for himself and a wool blanket for her. Wrapping it around her shoulders, he fought an insane desire to lift her into his arms and carry her to his quarters. That would be madness indeed.

He led the way to the boat and got underway in less than a minute. The clouds roiled overhead, but the rain had stopped and the wind had died. Lightning lingered over the mountain peaks, reaching down with jagged fingers to caress their dark outlines. He tried to remember if a storm had come up on the day his father went out on the lake—for whatever strange reason—with her mother.

"Was there a storm that day?" he asked.

She shook her head. "It was sunny, although a wind came up later. The police thought your father was somehow injured and my mother tried to sail the boat back to the dock. She failed to duck when the boom swung across in the wind."

"And was knocked out."

"Yes."

He cut the engine and coasted smoothly up to her pier, then grabbed the post and held the boat steady so she could climb out. She paused and gazed at him before dropping the blanket in the boat, then headed up the path across the broad sweep of lawn.

Watching her long-legged stride take her away from him, he struggled with another odd impulse to grab her back, to hold her and keep her safe from whatever demons lingered in the depths of her eyes. There was something alone and lonely within her that called to something within him.

And he didn't have the foggiest idea what it was.

Megan locked the door behind her when she entered the house. She checked the other entrances, making sure the dead bolts were in place before going to her room. Even with those precautions, she still didn't feel safe.

The problem was within herself, she admitted, as shivers chased along her spine. *He* was the problem. No, it was her own emotions when she was around him. He stirred longings she didn't need and had no time for. And somehow he was part of the nightmares and the fears they generated.

What was she afraid of?

No answer came to her. After a shower, she slipped into brushed-satin pajamas and dried her hair.

Going to the kitchen, she felt in control of her body and her thoughts once more.

Emotionally, she was still a little shaky, but a bowl of hot soup restored her spirits and rekindled her determination to face the past and get on with her life. She watched a movie, then went upstairs shortly after ten.

Across the way, she saw the lights go out in the main part of the house, then others come on in the wing closest to the National Forest property that separated the two ranches at the end of the lake.

On an impulse, she clicked off the lamp in her room, then turned it on again. On the other side of the lake, the light went out, then came back on.

Clamping both hands to her bosom, she backed away from the window. She slumped to the bed as her legs buckled and waves of shocked pleasure rushed over her. Laughter bubbled out of her. She felt like a child with a delightful secret, sending secret messages back and forth with a friend.

After a moment, she sobered. Kyle wasn't her friend. She'd better remember that.

"Shannon was wondering about you," Rory said shortly after arriving the next morning. "You two usually talk every day."

Megan smiled at her business partner and new cousin-in-law. "Me intrude on newlyweds? Heaven forbid."

His quiet smile of contentment brought a pang to her heart. She wanted the couple to be happy, of course she did, but she was envious of that happiness.

Feeling small and mean-spirited, she went over the breeding program with him. They were pleased with the new filly out of their best mare.

''Her conformation looks good,'' he commented on the young one, studying her lines as she stood in the pasture near her mother. ''Look at those legs. She'll make a show jumper for sure.''

''Let's not count our chickens before they hatch,'' she advised, laughing at his enthusiasm.

The vet smiled, then studied her for a minute. ''Kate says you and Kyle are trying to bring up the wreck of his father's sailboat.''

''Yes.''

With their arms crossed and resting on the top rail of the fence, they were silent as they contemplated the pastoral scene before them.

''Do you think we shouldn't?'' she finally asked.

''I don't know,'' he admitted, a thoughtful frown on his handsome face. ''Shannon worries about you suddenly getting your memory back.''

''She's afraid I'll be hurt.''

Rory shook his head. ''You'll have to face the truth, no matter what it is, but she doesn't want you to be alone when it happens. She thinks—''

''What?'' Megan asked when he stopped.

He gave her a worried look. ''You know, it was probably a traumatic event that blocked your memory, one you don't want to remember. She doesn't want you to face it alone.''

"I've already accepted that," she admitted as the familiar sadness darkened the brightness of the day. "I'm not that child. I can face whatever it is."

He gave her a pat on the back. "I think so, too. The Windom cousins are three of the bravest people I know."

"Well, the most stubborn," she conceded, striving for a lighter tone.

"That goes without saying."

They laughed and went inside the pasture. After he checked their breeding stock, he took off to the office and Megan got busy. Mondays were long, hard days, filled with training sessions and riding lessons. At noon, she heard the sound of an engine that she recognized.

Kyle pulled in at the dock as she was eating a sandwich while perched on the pasture railing. "You ready to try again?" he called as he crossed the lawn.

She shook her head. "Too busy today."

He climbed on the fence and observed the horses in the near pastures, then the cows in the meadow. Mr. Roddey, who leased several hundred acres of flat land from the ranch, was cutting hay again. The storm of the preceding day had hardly produced enough moisture to settle the dust, much less interfere in ranching operations.

"Then I guess I'll have to go alone."

"I wouldn't advise it."

"Why not?"

She prepared herself for his anger. "Because the lake is actually in the public domain and you have to have a permit from the forestry service to use it for more than recreational purposes."

His laser glare could have cut through steel plate. "When did you find out about this?"

"The day I got the compressor. I went right over and got the permit. It's in my name."

"And you saw no reason to impart this information to me."

From the edges of her vision, she saw the muscles tense in his jaw. "No," she admitted.

"I wonder sometimes what you're trying to hide."

His voice was so soft, she had to strain to catch the words. Indignation flew over her. "Not a thing. Like you, I only want to know the truth."

"Or to cover it up."

When he turned to her, she met his gaze without a qualm. "My family has nothing to hide."

"Neither does mine."

"Fine. The boat going down must have been an accident, an error on your father's part in sailing it."

His gaze honed in on her as he leaned closer. "Jimmy Herriot was an expert sailor. He didn't make mistakes."

She refused to back down. "Then how do you explain what happened?"

He didn't speak for a long minute, then, "Your father found them together, went into a rage and hit them with something, whatever came to hand. Thinking they were both dead, he sailed the boat into the rocks, scuttled it, then returned to shore—"

"How?" she demanded.

Kyle shrugged. "He could have tied the dory on behind, or maybe he swam. He was a strong swimmer. I saw him and your mother swim all the way across the lake once. They were racing. He let her win."

Megan turned to the lake, its waters placid and inviting. She envisioned two people swimming side by side while she watched from the pier, ready to declare the winner when they returned. She'd been happy and excited over being the official timekeeper. Her father had given her his watch and showed her how to set the timer. Her grandfather had been on the patio, fury in his eyes—

Megan gasped. The image disappeared.

She turned on Kyle. "My father wouldn't hurt anyone! He wouldn't! He was gentle and caring and...and...he loved my mother. He wouldn't have hurt her."

"Maybe," was all Kyle said.

"You think you have this all figured out," she accused, "but you don't. What if it was *your* mother who went into a jealous rage at finding her husband with another woman? What if she picked up an oar and started beating them?"

"A woman wouldn't be strong enough to bash in a man's ribs and knock someone unconscious."

"People can have superhuman strength at times. One woman lifted a car off her husband's chest when it fell on him. He crawled out from under it with only a couple of broken ribs."

"My mother didn't do it."

''Neither did my father.''

''So we're back to square one. Who attacked them, then scuttled the boat?''

''A stranger?'' she suggested. ''Someone who wanted to rob them.''

''Why would a stranger go to the trouble of sinking the boat? He'd take what he wanted and get out before someone came along and spotted him.''

She admitted a robbery wasn't likely. Nothing on the boat had been missing as far as anyone knew. Jimmy Herriot's wallet had been in his pocket. Her mother's engagement ring had been on her finger.

''It's a mystery,'' Megan admitted. ''One nobody has solved yet.'' She dared him to say differently.

Kyle jumped down from the fence, his face grim, his expression as haunted as her dreams. ''And after fifteen years, you and I are going to?'' He walked off.

''Yes,'' she whispered after he'd cast off and was on his way back to his side of the lake. The premonition was strong in her, as real as the sunlight glinting off the clear water. ''Yes...''

Chapter Eight

Tuesday morning, Megan called Shannon, then Kate. She chatted with each of them about their days and reported on her own, including the activity on the salvage operation.

"Which is a big zero at the present," she concluded.

"Are you and Kyle going out today?" Kate asked.

"I suppose so. After I get the chores done."

Kate was silent for a minute, then, "We could probably afford to hire some help. You work too hard. Jeremy will be gone all month."

The boy was in Houston, visiting with his mother and stepfather during the summer. He loved working with the horses and came over as often as he could. He'd been a big help to Megan during the school year and early summer.

"Nonsense. I hardly have enough to keep me out of mischief from day to day."

On that sardonic note, the cousins laughed and said goodbye. Megan had barely hung up when the phone rang. A frisson rushed along her scalp. "Windraven Ranch," she answered and heard the wariness in her voice.

"It's the big, bad wolf," Kyle said. "Is Little Red Riding Hood available?"

"Why? You want to eat her all up?"

His sarcastic laughter rang over the line. "Yeah, but I haven't time today. When are you going to be ready to go?"

"Um, around eleven. I'll meet you at the rock."

"All right." There was a pause. "What have you told Shannon and Rory about us?"

Her mind went blank. "Nothing that I know of. Why?"

"Rory stopped by yesterday. He told me to take good care of you. Or else."

"Or else what?"

"He didn't say. I suppose the implication was that your relatives will gang up on me if I don't treat you right."

The day suddenly seemed brighter at the wry humor evident in his tone. "I hope you'll remember that and act accordingly."

"Hey, I'm the injured party here," he objected.

"In what way?"

"Loss of sleep. Disturbing dreams when I do manage a few winks. A permanent state of, uh, tension."

Megan ignored the heat that ran up her neck and all the way to her hairline. "Don't tease," she said, feeling the situation between them was too raw to joke about. She, too, had spent a restless night.

"All right. See you at eleven."

She lingered for a few minutes after she hung up. He couldn't sleep for thinking of her? That funny electrical sensation buzzed through her nerve endings. She shivered and wrapped her arms across her chest, suddenly lost in dreams that weren't frightening at all.

The phone rang again. A mother wanted to know if she had an opening for her daughter in a riding class. Megan told her a beginners' class would be starting in the fall and took the child's name and age for inclusion.

Thinking of the coming season, she wondered what changes the summer would bring to her life. An answer to the questions that troubled her past? A passion that would sweep her into a future she'd never imagined?

An affair with her enemy was the way to foolishness. She didn't need to add that item to her to-do list. But, she mused, touching her lips and remembering how wild a kiss could be, it would be something to remember, something sweet and warm for cold winter nights....

"You're late," was Kyle's greeting when she joined him at the granite slab.

"I do run a riding academy," she reminded him.

She sighed. ''Everyone suddenly wants her child to become an Olympic champion in ten easy lessons.''

He tossed her the wet suit. She grimaced, but stripped down to her bathing suit and pulled on the too-tight outfit. With the hood in place, she hefted the air tanks onto her back and pulled the goggles over her head.

After checking her equipment, then his, Kyle signaled they were ready to go down. They clipped the miner's lights to their hoods. They would need those.

The water seemed even colder than usual as Megan sank into its depths. She saw that the boat had shifted again. Small rocks were scattered along the deck, indicating another rock slide. She worried about the granite slab and its many fissures, plus the load of broken rocks that sat atop it. If the slab should tilt a bit more, the rocks would rain down on the wreck, perhaps trapping them there.

When Kyle started clearing the deck of the debris, she did, too. Finished, he led the way into the hold. They explored each area thoroughly, finding life preservers, a box of flares, waterproof matches and flashlights in a storage compartment. Rusting cans, the paper wrappers detailing the contents long gone, lined the galley shelves.

A feast for ghosts.

She pushed the morbid thought into the recesses of her mind and watched her partner while he pried open the cover to the hold. Cold rushed over her as a current of icy water swept through the hole in the hull and the opening in the compartment.

Kyle directed the beam of his light into the bilge space and, gently using his flippers to hold his position, he peered inside. To her surprise, he pushed his head into the narrow space as far as he could. Panic seized her and she grabbed him by the ankle.

He backed out, then peered intently at her. She pointed upward, needing to get out of the wreck before something dire happened to them as it had their parents.

With a surprisingly gentle motion, he touched her shoulder, then under her chin. Holding up one finger to indicate one more minute, he went back to his exploration. Sticking one arm in the hold, he probed, then brought out a long, thick wedge of granite that tapered to a blunted end that might once have held a sharp point.

She stared at the wedge and saw it as a weapon...one of death and destruction.

Kyle pointed her toward the surface. They went up side by side, but not touching. As soon as they were standing on the granite slab and had shed the tanks, she held out her hand. "Let me see."

He handed over the piece of rock without a word.

"Do you think this went through the hull and caused the boat to go down?"

"Yes."

She surveyed the massive slab. "Was it attached to the granite here and did it break off when the sailboat hit?"

"That's possible, but I think it was used deliberately. Someone pounded the hull to make a hole large enough to sink the yacht as quickly as possible.''

''Someone,'' she repeated.

She removed the wet suit with an effort. He did the same with his. The dark granite was warm under her feet. The sun radiated warmth on her back as she faced him.

He watched her warily, but otherwise with no expression on his face.

''It wasn't my father,'' she said, sounding as if she were a long way off and listening to the conversation by some trick of acoustics.

Pity flickered through his eyes.

She shook her head. ''It wasn't.''

He lifted his hand as if he would comfort her.

''He was the gentlest person,'' she said, backing away from his touch, unable to bear it that he would accuse and comfort at the same time. ''He would never have hurt my mother. Never.''

She heard the uncertainty in her voice. Turning, she ran…from him, from herself, from the fear that clawed at her as if it would open her chest and rip out her heart.

''Megan,'' Kyle said.

But she didn't stop. She leaped into the dory, causing it to sway wildly. Holding on with one hand, she yanked the cord with the other. The engine roared to life.

Without looking back, she cast off and headed across the lake at full speed, her eyes strangely blinded, as if a mist had fallen over the lake, making everything blurry and unreal. It matched the way she felt inside.

At her house, she ran up the lawn and into the house. On the stairs, she had the eerie feeling someone was running with her, someone who was sobbing aloud, someone who was very, very frightened.

She stopped and listened, but heard only the sound of her own breath. She turned her head quickly, trying to catch the sound, and heard only the echoing footsteps of a child who had come this way fifteen years ago.

Legs trembling, Megan sank onto the top step. Grasping the balusters with both hands, she rested her head against them and closed her eyes tightly.

"Come back," she whispered hoarsely to the child. "Don't be afraid. Tell me what you know. Please. Tell me. I need to know."

She waited. There was no answer.

Kyle closed the window against the night chill. He pulled on a pair of jeans, then resumed his watch, his nerves on edge.

Sleep was impossible tonight. He kept hearing Megan's denial, kept seeing her run from him. She'd been frightened to the point of panic as she fled across the lake.

Why?

The question beat at him, had roiled within as he tried to sleep. He'd finally given up and stood at the window, staring at the dark outline of the house across the way.

He was tempted to go over there and shake the truth out of her. She was concealing something from him. Maybe from herself, too. Maybe the truth was too frightening—

His thoughts were interrupted by a light suddenly appearing across the lake. Megan's room. She was awake.

Without giving himself time to think, he pulled on a fleece shirt, jammed his feet into jogging shoes and without lacing them, set out for the dock. A few minutes later, he stood on Megan's patio, his hands at his sides while he tried to talk himself out of knocking.

She ended the debate by unlocking and opening the door. "I heard the boat," she said.

"You were already awake. I saw your light."

"The nightmare," she said wearily, "it's back. I've had it since...since I was eleven."

He entered the dark living room. "Tell me about it, everything. Don't leave out any detail."

She walked toward the hall. "I've put on coffee."

He followed her to the kitchen where a night-light gleamed softly over the sink. The scent of fresh coffee was normal and reassuring.

While they sipped the hot brew, she told him of the dream she'd been having for years, about the woman crying, and the girl—herself—who ran up the stairs, too frightened to speak, and hid in the closet until her father coaxed her out. "His eyes were so sad...so very sad...all red, as if he'd been crying, too," she ended.

Her sorrow was so profound, it pierced all the way to that sensitive place inside. "That's all? You don't know what caused the fright?" he asked as gently as he could.

She shook her head. "It's all mixed up—my father and grandfather shouting, my mother crying, then there's a terrible silence before the ravens start—"

"The ravens?"

"I think I'm running from them. They're chasing me and screeching over my head." She stopped and considered. "I just remembered that. It's part of the dream. The ravens always mean death."

"That's all, the ravens come, then the dream ends?"

She nodded. "I think so. I don't remember more."

"Did finding that granite wedge cause the nightmare?"

"No. I've been having it lately. Sometimes, around this time of year, it comes back. Today, fifteen years ago—"

Reaching across the table, he took her hands. "Don't think about it anymore. You need to rest."

"Why are you being kind? If what you suspect is true, then my father...my father..."

"Hush," he said. He rose and went around the table. When she stood and looked at him, any thought for self-preservation fled. There was only the need. Hers, and his.

He folded her into his arms.

She laid her head on his chest, then sighed, her arms creeping around him hesitantly.

"Don't be afraid," he said, and didn't have a clue as to why he said it, or what he meant.

"I'm not, not of you," she whispered. "Only myself. And all the things that might have been."

He turned her face up to his and kissed her. Her lips trembled under his, and he was lost to everything but them and the moment and the passion and the incredible longing to know her to the fullest, to ease the troubled pain he saw in her eyes and make her world safe again.

The kiss was endless. It spoke of all the things they couldn't say—the attraction of a man and woman toward each other, as natural as the rising sun; the fulfillment of passion, forbidden to them by family loyalty; the knowledge that they were enemies, separated by a river of grief.

The kiss changed, shifting from muted agony and a need to comfort to the pounding waves of desire between two creatures at their physical prime. He felt the change in her as her lips opened, and her tongue met his without shyness or coyness or any of the multitude of games humans played.

His heart nearly exploded.

His hands, and hers, caressed, grasped, clung to clothing, then an incredible flash of heat spread through him as she slipped her hands under his top and rubbed urgently along his back, pressing him closer.

He tried, honestly tried, to think, but only one thought formed in his mind. "Where?" he asked hoarsely.

"Upstairs. My room," she answered.

Lifting her into his arms, he carried her up the steps, his gaze restlessly exploring her face, her mouth....

In the bedroom, he let her slide to the floor, then held her against him, pounding heart to pounding heart.

"This could be dangerous," she said.

"For both of us," he agreed.

Megan nodded. In that instant, she knew what she was doing, what she wanted, what she intended to take. There was only one question she had to ask.

"Do you have...?" She considered what word she should use.

He made it easy for her. "Protection? Yes."

She drew back and looked up at him.

His eyes were dark, black instead of gray, in the dim light of her bedroom. "I knew it would come to this between us. I didn't want to be..."

"Foolish," she supplied.

He smiled slightly. "Caught off-guard," he corrected gently. "The foolishness I can't help."

A smile bloomed in her, too, the forerunner of an odd burst of happiness she couldn't suppress or explain. "Kiss me again," she whispered.

"My pleasure."

He was marvelous with his lips, drawing exclamations of surprise from her as he tasted her lips and neck, then licked a damp trail to a point between her breasts. The human body contained more erotic points than she had ever read about.

Her robe disappeared, then her pajama top. His hands were cool, then hot on her skin. Breathing became difficult, then unnecessary.

He stopped and gazed down at her, letting her catch up on the need for air. "Bed?"

She nodded and turned toward the four-poster. He lifted her onto it, then held the covers and urged her to lie back. The rest of her clothing disappeared, tossed behind him like so much flotsam in the turbulent sea of their desire.

She pushed the pillows against the headboard and observed as he undressed, first the fleece shirt, then his shoes, finally the jeans. He wore nothing underneath.

"You must have been cold, coming across the lake," she said, then wondered about his arrival. "Why did you come?"

"I couldn't sleep. When I saw your light come on, I..." He laughed softly, with irony. "I guess I didn't think. I just reacted."

"Because you knew I needed you?"

He considered, then shook his head. "Because I need you."

The statement was delivered lightly, but she felt its impact clear down to the center of her being. A brightness grew in that dark spot and sent warmth to every part of her body. She held out her arms. "Come to me."

Kyle lifted the covers and slipped into the comfortable bed. "I never expected to be here—" He stopped before he finished the thought.

''In your enemy's house?''

''In your bed.'' He kissed her eyes closed, then kissed her mouth open. Her body was like fine materials—silk and satin and velvet.

Megan couldn't get enough of the touching, the feel of skin on skin, the smooth surfaces, the rough textures of his masculine body. All seemed magical, intriguing to her touch.

There came a moment when this touching wasn't enough. ''Please,'' she murmured. ''Oh, please.''

He became more intimate, startling a gasp from her when he moved over her, then stroked her with slow, seductive movements of his body against hers.

''I feel as if I'll burst into flames,'' she said.

''I already have. You make me burn.''

He laid his head beside hers on the pillow and branded kisses along her temple and neck, then her lips. She writhed under him, pushing for more... more...

''If I touched you...here...''

He showed her, and she gave a low moan of pleasure.

''Yes, sing for me,'' he whispered. ''I want to hear your passion. I want to feel you come apart in my arms.''

''Will you do the same?'' she wanted to know, eager to understand his desire as well as her own.

''Darling, I'm already halfway there.''

''Then why don't you come to me?'' she invited, smiling up at him, feeling fierce and happy at the same time.

"One minute." He moved away from her, muttering a curse as he searched for his jeans and couldn't find them.

She switched on the lamp beside the bed to its softest glow and watched as he prepared himself.

Kyle glanced at her and smiled at her obvious curiosity. She was used to ranch life and breeding, but she brought an innocence to their love play that excited him more than the most practiced of courtesans ever could.

When he returned to her, she reached for him with an eagerness that caused an upheaval inside him, making him want to be fierce and gentle at the same time. He gritted his teeth when she reached for him.

"Easy," he warned. "I'm close to the edge."

"So am I."

He grinned at her openness, but knew she wasn't where he wanted her to be, not yet. But she would be soon.

Easing into position, he kissed her mouth, then her breasts until she was once again writhing beneath him. He stroked her eager flesh until her demands became vocal. Then he entered her slowly and carefully, working his way downward with gentle strokes until they were fully united.

She gazed up at him, her eyes dark and fathoms deep, like magic pools hidden within an enchanted forest. A floodgate of feelings opened within him.

"Megan," he said and didn't know what he wanted to say.

"Oh, Kyle, that feels...I can't describe..."

When she lifted to him, all thought disappeared as wildfires erupted all through him.

Megan felt the momentary struggle in him, then the triumphant need as they moved together, feeding each other with their passion, moving faster, more intently. She felt him tense, then thrust once more. A shudder raced over him and into her, joining them in the moment.

She cried out as the peak came, sweeping her up like a tidal wave until she was saturated with sensation, then setting her gently down on a sandy beach of contentment.

His weight on his arms, he rested over her for several minutes. She caressed his back, mindlessly sated, feeling she would never move again. When he rolled to the side, he turned her with him. She snuggled against his chest and planted a string of kisses wherever she could reach.

She was nearly asleep when she felt him shift. She opened her eyes and saw him watching her. She was surprised to find she wasn't in the least self-conscious about their passion. "Are you leaving?"

He hesitated. "Do you want me to?"

"No."

His chest moved under her cheek. "Then I won't."

"Good. I don't want to be alone."

Raising up on an elbow, he studied her. "Sex as an antidote for nightmares?" he questioned.

"For loneliness." As his eyes darkened, she added, "Or maybe it was just for itself, a moment beyond time and worldly cares.'' She considered. ''Yes, I think that was it.''

He seemed almost sad. ''It was mind-blowing, but the world always returns afterwards.''

''We don't have to think about it now.'' She patted his chest, then rubbed soothingly up and down his torso. Even now, surfeited with physical sensation, she found she loved touching him.

He disposed of the condom, reached across her and turned off the lamp. Lying on his back, he wrapped an arm around her and drew her close.

After a minute, he spoke. ''I've never stayed all night with a woman.''

''You make love, then get up and leave?''

''We have sex, then I leave.''

She wondered if, by staying, he was admitting to making love. A faint alarm pinged through the drowsiness. They'd had more than sex, but love? It was out of the question.

It was an odd thing filled with pleasant surprises, this waking up with a woman in his arms, Kyle found. He lay cupped around Megan's slender frame, her rump tucked into his groin as if they'd snuggled this way for years.

Slowly, enjoying the tactile sense to the fullest, he slid his hand over her arm, back, side, then upward to cup her breast. It beaded against his palm.

His body sprang to attention in an instant.

Shaking his head as if to tell his libido to be still,

he continued caressing her, moving to the smooth curve of her hip and along her thigh to her knee.

She took a deep breath, but didn't wake. He nuzzled his face into her hair, inhaling the warm essence of her. He'd wanted to touch those fiery auburn tresses for a long time. He liked the silkiness of them and the tangles from sleeping and from their lovemaking. Using his fingers, he combed them into a semblance of order, but not too much.

A hand glided over his hip, causing him to tense. She followed a meandering trail along his thigh, then his abdomen. The air hung in his lungs. When she touched him intimately, he managed to breathe once more.

Brushing the hair aside, he kissed her neck and up to her ear. When he nibbled on the lobe, she laughed.

"Maybe I'd better feed the beast," she suggested.

"I think you're going to have to." But he wasn't talking about food. When she turned to him, he asked, "Are you okay?"

She nodded and caressed his cheek. "Rough."

"I'll be careful," he promised. "Stay here."

He swung out of bed, went down to the kitchen and put on a pot of coffee. Bringing a glass of orange juice, he returned upstairs. She came out of the bathroom, her hair combed and swinging around her shoulders.

"We're just going to mess it up again," he advised, bringing the glass to her mouth.

After she drank, he did, too. They shared the juice until it was gone. He set the glass on the table.

''Seven.'' He noted the time. ''It's been ages since I slept this late.''

''Me, too. The horses are probably wondering what's happening.''

''This,'' he murmured, bending forward to kiss her breasts into erect points. ''This is what's happening.''

Megan found making love in the morning was as exciting as at night. When she and her lover were sated, she lay on top of him and listened to his heart rate slow.

''Ohh,'' she groaned when her stomach growled for the second time. ''Time for food.''

She washed and dressed, then went to the kitchen. After pouring a cup of coffee, she prepared toast and eggs.

''This looks great.'' Kyle helped himself to coffee.

He took a seat when she did. They ate without conversation. Watching the shadows recede over the pastures as the sun climbed higher, she wondered where they would go from here. ''What happens next?''

''Between us?''

She nodded as he spread homemade jelly on the last piece of toast, cut it in two and handed half to her.

His expression went bleak, as if the sadness had returned. ''I intend to keep on working on the wreck. I still want to know the truth.''

She ate the toast, then wiped her mouth. ''You

think someone used that granite wedge to pound a hole in the hull of the boat.''

It wasn't a question, but he nodded anyway.

She looked down at her plate. ''So do I,'' she admitted in a low voice. ''But it wasn't my father.''

The handsome planes of his face shifted subtly, becoming harder, unrelenting. ''Then who?'' he asked.

''I don't know. I just don't know.''

He stood. ''Neither do I, but I'll find out.''

''How?''

''I think you're the key. If you could remember that day.''

A shudder ran from her head to her feet, dispelling the warmth of their night together, leaving her chilled and worried. She lifted her chin. ''I will,'' she vowed.

He nodded, hesitated, then surprised her by touching her hair gently before going out the back door into the cool morning.

Chapter Nine

When Mrs. Roddey appeared at nine, Megan was surprised. The wife of the man who leased the hay fields, Mrs. Roddey had often helped her take care of her grandfather, cook and clean—whatever was needed. She'd asked the quiet, efficient woman to come over and help her clean house once a month. The rest of the time she picked up after herself.

"Come on in," she called, dredging up a smile as she rose from the computer where she was updating the ranch records and went into the kitchen. "I'd forgotten which day we were going to clean."

"The third Wednesday of each month." Mrs. Roddey reminded her. "Here, I brought you some rolls."

Megan inhaled deeply. "Mmm, cinnamon, my favorite.'' She plucked one out of the bag and took a big bite. For an odd second, this small act of kindness threatened her composure. ''Why did we pick the third Wednesday?''

''It's the day Ralph visits his mother.''

''Oh, that's right.'' After a moment, she spoke. ''Mrs. Roddey, do you recall the day of the boating accident, the day my mother drowned?''

Mrs. Roddey paused in getting the vacuum from the closet. She nodded.

''Where was I? It was summer. Was I at home?''

''Yes, you were here.'' She clicked the wand attachment into place. ''I saw you that day, swinging upside-down on a limb in the big oak when I brought Ralph's lunch to him.''

Megan gazed toward the tree. It grew at the far end of the lawn, near the lake's edge. She'd made her own space up there, nailing boards across two limbs to form a seat. Some part of her knew that, but she couldn't remember ever having played in it. Years later, looking up into the massive branches, she'd recalled the rickety platform. It was gone and she didn't know what had happened to it.

Like cold fingers along her back, an echo of past fear shivered through her. ''I used to play there.''

''It was your favorite place,'' Mrs. Roddey agreed. ''When you weren't on a horse.'' Smiling, she wheeled the vacuum cleaner to the living room and began cleaning.

Megan continued staring at the oak for another minute. With a mental shake, she got busy changing the sheets in her bedroom. The blood thrummed heavily through her body as she caught Kyle's scent mingled with her own. She quickly thrust the linens in the washer, including the damp towels from their showers.

While getting the house in order, she mused on the strange contentment of the night. Had it been wrong to find pleasure in the arms of her enemy?

Maybe not, but it had been foolish. It was a memory that hummed, fresh and vibrant, through her as she worked the morning away.

At noon, she thanked Mrs. Roddey, paid her for her work and said goodbye. Then she set out for the rocky island near the end of the lake. Kyle's powerboat was already there.

She sat on the warm granite and waited.

Kyle came up and removed his wet suit, pulled on a pair of old cutoffs over his trunks and settled on the rock near her. "I think I'm ready to try bringing the boat up. I've screwed a cover over the hole. We can pump air into the hold, then the forward cabin. The water should drain out the back."

"All right." She tried not to be aware of him, sitting no more than two feet away, his chest bronzed by the sun, the dark curly hairs glinting in the bright light.

He cocked an eyebrow at her. "No argument?"

"No."

"You're quiet today. Was it something I did?" His half smile was teasing, but his eyes were serious.

She shook her head and stared intently at the

mountain that rose abruptly from the edge of the water and soared to ten thousand feet.

He probed further. "Regrets? Second thoughts?" With a finger under her chin, he turned her head to his, forcing her to meet his eyes.

"No. I wish the night could have lasted forever." She managed a smile, but her heart felt low, as if being tugged into the silent, icy world under the lake.

His pupils dilated, causing his eyes to go black. He leaned toward her, his gaze on her mouth.

She turned her head, shaking it slightly to cast off the foolish longing.

"My God, woman, you tell me that and expect me to keep my hands off you?" he murmured, catching her face between both his hands.

"What good is passion?" she asked and felt the forlorn melancholy she'd experienced while they'd waltzed at her cousin's wedding.

"It proves a point," he said in a low, husky tone that caused her throat to knot up. "I think the attraction could be serious between us." He paused. "I think you feel the same."

"We're enemies," she reminded him in fierce denial.

"Partners," he corrected, his fingers sliding into her hair and holding her captive. His eyes devoured her.

She pulled away from him and all the bright hopes he raised in her. "We don't want complications, remember?" she demanded, gathering anger, her only defense, around her like a ragged, scratchy cloak.

He let her go and stuffed his uneaten sandwich in the bag. "Yeah, I remember," he said, regret underscoring the words. "Do you?"

Stung, she asked, "What does that mean?"

"Do you really not recall the past? Or are you protecting those near and dear to you?"

"My father," she surmised.

"Yes. Sean Windom had motive and opportunity. He was at home that day."

She put her hands to her head.

"I checked. He didn't register any cattle for sale at the auction as he told the police. There's no evidence he was even there."

"He was."

Kyle pulled her hands from over her ears. "Where was he?" he asked with dogged determination. "If he had nothing to hide, why did he lie?"

Blackness whirled inside her head. She fought it off, desperately needing all her senses about her. The nightmare closed in. The ravens cawed restlessly, as demanding as the man who pushed for answers she desperately wished she could give.

"I don't know. I don't remember."

"Or won't," he said grimly.

The nightmare rushed at her. The ravens beat at her head. She was cold, so cold, all of a sudden. Twisting her head around, she forced herself to face them, to look at the darkness inside the dream and see the truth.

Two black birds landed on a boulder behind her.

They cocked their heads and stared back at her. One, braver than the other, flew at them.

"Git," Kyle said and waved his arm.

The two birds took off for the trees at the shore, their indignant cries echoing off the granite cliffs at the end of the lake.

Megan blinked and reality returned. She wasn't having a nightmare. The ravens were real. So was the moment. And the pain. It hurt that he distrusted her, but then, she had known he had the power to hurt her. She'd known that from the opening beat of the waltz when he'd held her in his arms for the first time. The truth could hurt both of them.

"What do we have to do to float the sailboat?" she asked, putting emotion at bay. She drank deeply from the soda to relieve her dry mouth, then rose to get the wet suit from the locker on Kyle's boat.

"I talked to Jess. He'll come out on Saturday and give us a hand. With his experience, we stand a better chance."

"That's a good idea." She couldn't explain the relief that ran over her at the reprieve. "I suppose there's nothing to do until then?"

"Right."

He came over to her. Knowing he was going to kiss her, she stood still, taking it but not giving anything back. When he stepped away, his face was a mask that hid any emotion from her. So was hers.

"I'm tired," she said. "I'm going home."

He watched her leave without a word.

At the house, she prowled through the rooms until

she came to her grandfather's office. She'd done nothing in there for days. There were still drawers to go through. And the journals to be read.

However, she'd hardly sat down in the chair when she was interrupted. Shannon and Kate rushed into the house.

"Come on," Kate said. "There's a fire sale in town. We want to check out the bargains."

"They're going to burn down the place when everything's sold?" Megan joked, feeling far from humorous.

"Right," Shannon said. "Then we're going to have tea at Lady Charlotte's. Hurry up and dress."

Megan went to her room and changed into a golden-yellow peasant skirt and a white knit top with a garden of daisies printed around the bottom. Her spirits perked up. An afternoon of browsing around with two of her favorite people was just what the doctor ordered.

Kate drove them into town in her compact station wagon. She reported on Amanda, who was at a birthday party and spending the night with the birthday girl.

"This is her first night away from home," Kate told them. "She's delighted and I'm worrying myself sick."

"Parental separation anxiety," Shannon remarked gravely, then laughed. "Guess what? The county approved my appointment as head of family counseling. The state came through with the funds."

''Great. You'll be wonderful,'' Megan assured her cousin.

Shannon sighed. ''I hope so. I already have a roster of ten kids in detention. The judges want the family situations evaluated before they decide what to do about them.''

''That sounds wise,'' Kate said as she stopped, then pulled onto Main Street. She found a parking space and they all hopped out, ready to explore the sale.

Two hours later, Megan sank gratefully into a chair at the new tea shop in town. She saw it served sandwiches, salads, an assortment of cookies—listed as biscuits—and coffee, as well as every tea known to man.

''Chamomile will put you to sleep,'' Shannon advised. ''It's a relaxant. Very good before bed. Red hibiscus is delicious, full of bioflavonoids.''

''I want something sinful,'' Kate declared, her reading glasses perched on her nose.

''Me, too,'' Shannon echoed.

They decided on meringue cakes with fruit, drizzled with a purée of raspberry and sprinkled with pecans.

''Umm,'' Kate said after eating the rich dessert, ''that exactly hit the spot. I'd better not bring Jess and Jeremy here, or I'll never get them out.''

Megan gazed thoughtfully at her cousin. ''Speaking of Jess, he's going to help with the wreck Saturday, according to Kyle. We're going to try to bring the boat up.''

"Already?" Shannon exclaimed. "I didn't realize it would go so fast."

"Well, it isn't the *Titanic,*" Megan said with a smile. She sobered. "We've examined it pretty thoroughly. I don't think we'll learn anything from the yacht."

Shannon, a former police detective, was disappointed. "I'd hoped we could solve this case once and for all."

"Maybe we could—if I could remember that day. Mrs. Roddey said I was home. Kyle says my father wasn't at the cattle auction in Cheyenne."

"The police report says he was," Shannon informed them.

"Kyle checked. Dad didn't register as a seller."

"Maybe he sold the cattle before the auction started, in a private deal," Kate suggested.

"Maybe," Megan said. She glanced at Shannon, tension pulling at her. "There's something I've been thinking about. Do you think I could be hypnotized or whatever and made to remember the day of the accident?"

"Regression? That might work."

"Could you—"

Shannon shook her head vehemently. "I wouldn't even attempt it. I don't have enough experience, for one thing. For another, I'm a relative. I wouldn't be an unbiased interpreter of the experience. And something could happen."

"Like what?" Kate asked.

"Megan may have had a traumatic encounter. It

would be better to have someone else help her through it. But I'd gladly be there for moral support. Do you want me to set it up? We'd have to go to Cheyenne."

"Not yet. Not until the boat is brought up. Also, did I tell both of you I've found some old journals written by Grandmother Rose?"

"Really? Have you read them?" Shannon demanded.

"Only the first one. It started on her wedding day to Grandfather. She was excited and happy. She knew Mary Dee Sloan, of course. She mentioned the birth of Mary's son and then her own, six months later."

"She didn't say anything about the breakup between Mary Dee and Grandfather?" Kate asked.

"Not a word."

Shannon sighed. "I don't think we'll ever know for sure. I did some checking through old court records recently. Mary's brother did get arrested for cattle-rustling, then the charges were dropped." Shannon looked from one cousin to the other. "Right after her marriage to Sonny Herriot."

"Then the gossip was right on that one," Kate concluded. "Grandfather had such a temper. I remember him quarreling with Uncle Sean." She stopped and cast an apologetic glance at Megan.

"I know he and Dad had some pretty loud arguments," Megan admitted. "Mostly over Dad marrying someone not approved by Grandfather."

Kate grimaced. "It's sad, what we do to each

other, all in the name of the best of intentions. I'm sure Grandfather thought he was one hundred percent right in his choice of a bride for Uncle Sean."

"Because he wanted my father to be governor one day." Megan took a sip of tea. "I remember that. Why didn't he run for office himself if he wanted it so badly?"

"His temper?" Shannon suggested. "Everybody liked Uncle Sean. A lot of people carried grudges against Grandfather after being subjected to one of his tongue-lashings."

"Yet," Megan said, "he could be kind. And he was gentle with us girls."

"He was," Kate agreed. "He always had a treat for me when I went over to the big house. Once we rode for hours to observe an eagle's nest and see the aerial maneuvers of the mating pair. I've never forgotten the wonder of it."

The three of them were quiet after that, each lost in her own thoughts of the past. At last Megan reached for her purse. "I've got to get home and do the chores. This was a lovely treat."

"Now that my honeymoon is over, can we resume meeting for lunch?" Shannon asked, putting in her part of the check.

Laughing, they agreed they could. Outside, Shannon headed for the courthouse. She'd bum a ride home with Jess or her husband. Kate and Megan returned to the ranch in Kate's station wagon.

Once on the county road, Kate flicked a quick look

at Megan. "Are you okay? I've been worried since the wedding. You're quieter than usual."

"I'm fine. I think." Megan smiled, although the odd melancholy settled around her as they neared home. "Kate?"

"Mmm?"

As her cousin parked on the circular drive in front of the old mansion, Megan's gaze picked out the bits of flaking paint on the clapboards. The house was still impressive, but it was definitely past its prime. Paint and repairs cost money.

Kate switched off the engine and turned to her.

"Kyle thinks things could get serious between us," she blurted.

"Wow," Kate said softly. "Next time please send a notice when you're going to drop a bombshell."

"Well, here comes another. He spent the night."

Kate looked worried. "That does complicate things. Are you having second thoughts about a relationship with him?"

"I'm not sure we have a relationship. An attraction and there are...feelings, but..."

"There's the past."

"Yes. He thinks my father may have..." She just couldn't say the words.

"Killed Jimmy Herriot and Aunt Bunny," Kate finished for her. "I'm sure more than one person has speculated on that scenario."

It was one of the reasons she loved her cousin. Kate faced life in whatever form it came.

"He didn't," Kate stated.

"How can we be sure?"

Megan found it hurt to ask the question. It came to her that she was beginning to doubt her father, a thing she'd never allowed in the past.

Kate sighed and looked as sad as Megan felt. "I suppose we can't, other than knowing the man and his nature. Uncle Sean was a wonderful person."

"To us, but he and Grandfather used to quarrel. Over my mother and the marriage. Money. The ranch."

"Perhaps he should have left. Fathers can be so hard on their sons."

Megan pressed her fingertips to her temples. "Mother wanted to leave. I remember she was terribly unhappy...."

Kate watched her without speaking as the flicker of memory went through her mind.

"I think we were going to leave. Grandfather was furious. He accused my mother of plotting against him."

Suddenly the darkness beat at her, like a thousand ravens descending upon the car. She couldn't breathe, couldn't see...

"Megan? Are you all right?"

Megan focused on Kate's dear, familiar features—the beautiful blue eyes with their fringe of black lashes, the smooth pale skin and the halo of dark hair with its auburn highlights inherited from Grandmother Rose.

"Yes," she whispered, then more strongly, "yes,

of course. I was trying to recall a wisp of memory, but it's gone now."

Kate gave her a hug. "Try not to worry. Things have a way of working out."

"Even with one's enemy?"

"Enemies can fall in love."

"Like Romeo and Juliet? Look what happened to them."

Kate grinned at the wry tone. "Call me if you feel driven to drink a vial of poison. I may join you."

Megan was at once concerned. "Are you having troubles?"

"Jess's ex has decided she wants Jeremy back, and the child-support payments."

Megan muttered an expletive.

"Yeah. However, Jess made her sign over custody when she dumped Jeremy on him without notice and said she couldn't handle the boy anymore."

"I've found Jeremy to be a wonderful person. He's great with the horses, and he loves living here."

"I agree. We might have to go to court, but the lawyer is sure we have the stronger case. It's a worry, though."

"Life isn't fair. Not that anyone ever said it would be," Megan said, feeling guilty for worrying about a past that couldn't be changed, no matter what the truth was, when her cousin had serious problems in the here-and-now.

"We take it as it comes, a day at a time," Kate acknowledged, her smile in place once more.

Megan gave her cousin a hug and slid out of the

car. The mare whinnied upon catching her scent. She knew it was time for her bucket of oats.

Megan waved goodbye to Kate, then went inside to change clothes. She hadn't resolved the question of Kyle and their involvement at all, but she felt somewhat better. Kate didn't think she was an awful person for having slept with the enemy. Megan wasn't sure what *she* thought.

A frisson swept over her. Would he come over tonight? And if he did, should she invite him in?

Kyle threw the pizza box in the trash, tossed the beer bottle in the recycling bin and washed his hands. Rotating his shoulders, he went into the TV room to catch the news. It was late and he was tired.

Cattle prices were dismal and the weather was predicted to stay the same. The usual hot-spot countries were fighting. Nice to know the world was dependably insane.

After clicking off the set, he went to his quarters, which consisted of an office-sitting room, a large bedroom with a king-size bed and a bathroom that had once been used as a nursery.

He wondered if he'd ever have any kids to occupy the two empty bedrooms across the hall.

Pushing the idea into the recesses of his mind, he tossed off the sweats he'd donned after a shower, turned out the light and went to the window instead of the bed.

He recognized the lighted window across the way. Megan was still awake, or else she'd gone to sleep with the light on. There'd been no TV in her room, but bookshelves had been built into an alcove and were filled with volumes. He hadn't noticed the titles.

Because they'd been too busy making love.

He smiled slightly. He had no regrets in that regard, even though he agreed with Megan that it probably hadn't been a wise thing to do.

Thinking of her brought on the familiar surge of heat in his lower body. He saw the moon was full enough to guide him across the lake. Not that he needed much guidance. Her house was a straight shot from his. He could have found his way there through a fog.

With a sardonic snort at his own longing, he went to bed and, surprisingly, was soon asleep.

At ten minutes before midnight, he awoke. Sitting up, he perused the dark room, then noticed the light across the lake. Worry speared through him. Was something wrong at Megan's place?

Rising, he peered toward the hay barn, then the stables. No lights at those, so presumably she wasn't overseeing a birth.

The nightmares again? Was that what was keeping her awake? She'd slept fine in his arms last night. Right. Sex as a cure for bad dreams. So maybe she needed him....

Even as he dressed in warm clothing, he scoffed at his reaction. She'd probably think he was crazy, coming to check on her in the middle of the night.

He could call. But he didn't.

Ten minutes after he awoke, he was on his way

across the lake, the engine thrumming smoothly, its steady vibrations coming through the deck and soles of his shoes. He tied up at the Windom dock shortly after that.

A light came on in the kitchen, then the pier lights.

His heart jumped around in his chest like a startled deer. It didn't settle down all the way up the lawn and across the patio. He saw a shadow at the door, then it swung open, letting him in. It closed of its own accord, giving a small *click* as the lock snapped into place behind him.

"It's late," Megan said, glancing at the clock, then back to him. "Midnight."

"I know. I woke up, saw your light."

She made a small gesture with her hands, one of helplessness. "I couldn't sleep. I was reading."

"I thought you might be having bad dreams."

Her hand clasped the lapel of the robe she'd put on over the satiny pajamas. "No, no dreams."

"Good."

He took a step forward. She watched him without speaking, her slender face all big, dark eyes in the dim light. He hesitated, not wanting her to be afraid of him, and wondered why she stood so still.

When he took another step, she finally moved. Her arms circled his shoulders and she pressed her face against his chest. Relief made his knees weak, but only for a second, then he locked his arms around her and swung them around as joy, swift and exuberant, filled him like sunlight.

She clasped her legs around his hips and clung to

him, all sweet feminine delight. The scent of her made his head spin. At the top of the stairs, he kissed her and still managed to find her room without mishap.

They sank to the bed in a bundle of arms and legs, moving, twisting, pushing clothing out of the way, fighting to get close.

"Protection," he muttered on a groan of frustration and searched for the box he'd stuck in his pocket.

He heaved a pent-up breath when he was at last snug inside her, her legs locked around him again. He looked into her eyes while he thrust gently.

The deep green mist within their depths pulled him into her, his soul into hers, until he no longer knew where he ended and she started. It wasn't a thing he'd ever experienced before.

They kissed and touched and bit hungrily at each other. They made love as if they fought, seeking the closeness of the flesh that their spirits demanded. At last he could take no more.

"Now," he said and heard the desperation in the word. *"Now."*

"Yes. Yes, yes, yes, yes," she cried and stiffened beneath him. "Oh, yes."

It was one thing to make love to a woman, he discovered. It was another to completely lose yourself in her. A dangerous situation. Emotion, unwise and forbidden, rose stubbornly within him.

As they settled in each other's arms, sated and relaxed, she yawned, her eyes closed. Kyle sensed she was near sleep. The odd sadness came over him. Seeking a light tone, he murmured, "Sex as an antidote to insomnia. It might be a miracle cure."

A terrible tenderness clutched him at her smile. He wanted to protect her from all of life's hurts and knew he couldn't.

"It would be nice to think so," she finally said.

He thought there was sadness in her, too, the way there had been the night of the wedding. He held her closer and kissed her hair, her temple, then he, too, went to sleep.

Chapter Ten

The next morning, Kyle went home to do his chores while Megan did the same. Outside, after feeding those animals she was observing for one reason or another, she moved a small herd of heifers to another field for grazing and put a bull in with them to cover those who hadn't "taken" during the prior breeding session.

Later, seated on the patio, she gazed across the lake. The sun sparkled on the water like liquid pools of some magic stuff and cast diamond dust on each pine needle.

The sky was clear blue, except for a gathering of puffy clouds over the tallest peaks. Perhaps a thunderstorm would come through that afternoon.

The whicker of the mare to her newborn and the

plangent bellowing of a distant cow to her calf brought a lump to her throat. Life seemed precarious and precious all at once.

Because of the night?

Because of the man. Because she was in love with Kyle Herriot and because it felt futile and foolish. As futile as her grandfather's love for a woman he'd lost.

Grandmother Rose, in her journal, had wept because her husband had called her by the wrong name while they made love. Apparently he hadn't realized it. He had given her a magnificent necklace on their twentieth anniversary, though. Later, when she was dying, he told her how much he cherished her in a poem he'd written himself:

> A crimson rose for me? No,
> I'll take the shy one hidden
> Behind the arbor, and so shaded,
> Shines all the more brightly,
> Far beyond the flagrant blossoms that
> Gather and worship the sun.
> Rose, sweet Rose, of softest pink
> By nature, and quiet, a retreat
> For the weary soul. Mine.

Megan couldn't believe her grandfather would take the time to write such thoughts down, even if he did think them. She imagined her grandmother reading them and felt the sorrow in the other woman's heart at knowing she was not the love of his life. Yet the words were cherishing.

Had her grandfather realized almost too late how very much he loved his Rose?

Sighing, Megan returned to the chores of training the horses under her care and preparing a class plan. All was quiet across the way. Kyle wasn't going out in the boat today, he'd said earlier. They would wait until Saturday.

After a silent dinner, Megan selected the final set of the journals, written in the last years of her grandmother's life. Rose and one of her daughters, Kate's mother, had died of breast cancer. The three cousins kept a careful check on their own bodies because of that. She read until the final journal ended with Rose's prayers and blessings for her three children and their children, those born and those yet to come. Her last thought was for her husband:

"I wish you peace in your soul," she'd written, "and a lightness of the heart to last the rest of your days."

Shortly after eleven, filled with the gripping nostalgia that had haunted her of late, Megan settled into bed and snapped out the light. Kyle's house was dark, too. For a wild, heart-pounding moment, she thought of calling and inviting him over.

But sense prevailed. Both of them led busy lives. Neither had time for an affair. She forced her eyes closed.

When dawn broke, she groaned. Friday. It was another heavy day of lessons and training. Time to get on with it.

By evening, she was finished and pleasantly tired. The day's lessons had gone well. The gelding had stopped trying to take a plug out of her leg. No one had fallen off a horse. No one had cried in fright at being on one. No parent wanted to know why her child wasn't in an advanced class. All in all, a good day.

After updating the ranch books and entering the amounts she'd spent on feed and medicine in the journals so Kate, the accountant, wouldn't fuss, she went to her room.

Seeing the journals, she took them downstairs to her grandfather's office and stored them in the bookcases. Absently she gazed around the room. In the corner, the silver-headed cane and several types of walking sticks, presumably used by some of her ancestors, rested in a huge ceramic jar that had once been a pickle vat.

She examined each piece, but could see no sign that any of them had been used to bash anyone. Spying a shorter item, she pulled out a baseball bat.

Recognizing it as the old "Louisville Slugger" she'd had as a Little League member years ago, she looked it over. The many scrapes and dings reminded her of the days when she was determined to be the best hitter on her team. Both her parents had pitched endless balls to her, then fielded them so she could get lots of practice.

The darkness closed in without warning, accompanied by the sound of a thousand birds cawing. Their wings, flapping all around her, drowned out the gasp of fright as she slipped down...down...down...

Reaching out, she encountered the wall, grasped a picture frame, felt it hold, then give, as she clutched desperately at consciousness. She slid down to the floor.

She put her hands over her ears. The horrendous racket of the birds receded. Bending forward, she put her forehead against the carpet until the darkness faded. Finally, it and the noise were gone.

Although feeling slightly nauseated, she rose and, a hand to her forehead, tried to figure out what had happened. Her gaze fell on the bat. She instinctively knew some memory was associated with it.

"You have to face it," she whispered to the child she had once been. "You have to."

She replaced the Slugger in the jar and reached over to straighten the picture frame, but stopped without touching it, her eyes going wide. The frame had moved because it was hinged on one side. And there was a safe tucked into the wall behind it!

Giving a tug on the knob in the center of the combination lock, she found it securely fastened.

She glanced around the room as if expecting the combination to suddenly appear like the handwriting on the wall in biblical days. No such luck.

After considering, she tried several of the usual combos of numbers. Her grandfather's birthday. Her grandmother's. Father. Mother. Aunts. Cousins.

Wedding dates. December 7, 1941—Pearl Harbor day. Nothing worked.

"Easy," Jess said, although Kyle couldn't possibly hear. "Easy does it."

Megan tightened the rope she was handling to take out slack as the yacht rose slowly off the ledge. The compressor wheezed noisily, pumping air down a hose and into the hold of the sailboat. Kyle was down below, keeping an eye on the operation and making sure the hose stayed in place.

Kate, Shannon and Rory had also accompanied the other three to the granite island for the big event.

Suddenly, Kyle's head broke the water's surface. "It's coming," he called to them.

Bubbles boiled around him, then the bow of the yacht shot upward at a steep angle. With a lunge, the boat fell forward as the rest of it appeared on the top of the lake.

"All right!" Jess yelled.

Kate and Shannon clapped and cried out in delight. Rory gave Jess a high five, then clipped a line to the railing on the yacht and guided it parallel to the rocky ledge they stood on.

Kyle tossed his flippers into his powerboat. "Okay, we've got to get it moving before it sinks again. Let's head for home!"

The men secured lines to the yacht and attached them to the dory and the powerboat. Megan and Kyle cranked up the engines on the smaller boats. The cousins climbed in Kyle's boat while Jess and Rory pushed the two crafts off, then jumped in, Jess in Megan's dory, Rory with the others. They headed for Kyle's boathouse as fast as they dared.

Megan didn't draw a full breath until they had the waterlogged yacht safely in the boat slip. A canoe was stored on hooks attached to a rafter, she noted. Kyle had a pump to remove the rest of the water from the sailboat.

"Can it be saved?" Shannon asked, running a hand over the wooden railing.

"Sure," Kyle told her. "It's really in good condition."

"Considering the condition it's in," Jess added wryly.

The laughter eased the tension of their Saturday-morning expedition. They'd started the operation of raising the *Mary Dee* at nine. It was now past one.

Jess removed the cover Kyle had fixed over the hole. All of them studied it intently. Kyle showed them the wedge of granite. Jess noted that it fit exactly into a chipped place on the hull. A long moment of silent contemplation ensued as they examined the evidence.

Megan met Kyle's speculative look without flinching. She knew what he was thinking. Worse, she was thinking it, too. Unable to sustain his stare, she turned away.

"I'm starved," Shannon informed them.

Rory hooked an arm around his bride's neck. "This woman is eating me out of house and home."

"Let's raid the refrigerator," Kyle said. He

checked the pump, nodded that it was doing okay and led the way to his house. In the attractive modern kitchen, he set out deli meats, sourdough buns and condiments. The three men had beers while the women opted for sodas.

Megan kept a smile on her face as the rest of the crew talked about the sailing ship and how difficult it would be to restore it. The news of the safe burned in the back of her mind. She wasn't ready to share the information.

Scared? she chided herself.

Yes, the answer came right back at her.

"What do you want to do with the yacht?" Kate asked, breaking into Megan's introspection. "After all, it's half yours, isn't it? Isn't that the law of salvage?"

"Yes," Kylc said when she failed to answer. "I thought we'd have it appraised, then I'd offer to buy Megan out."

Her gaze jerked to his. She hadn't thought of that possibility. They hadn't discussed it before now.

Because they'd either been making love or quarreling about her father's guilt.

"I didn't figure it would have anything but monetary value to you," he explained.

The hurt that only he could inflict spiraled down to the place that only he had ever breached. "It doesn't mean anything to me," she said coolly. "Except for what it can tell us about what happened."

"Someone definitely scuttled the yacht," Jess told them, putting a thick sandwich on a plate and grabbing a handful of chips from the bag. "But it can't tell us who."

"Or why," Rory added.

"If I could remember," Megan began, then stopped as all eyes turned her way. "But I don't."

Kate patted her arm. "Don't worry. It really doesn't matter. Well, it doesn't," she said defensively as Kyle cast a hard glance her way.

"Kate's right," Jess agreed. "At this late date, knowing exactly what happened, or even why it happened, won't change a thing."

"Except settle the questions in the minds of the living," Shannon said in a musing tone. She sighed and stood. "I have work to do this weekend. I have to give a report to the county commission on Monday about my expectations for the family counseling service."

"Good luck," Kate said sympathetically. She glanced at her watch. "We have to go, too. Amanda is visiting a friend. It's time to pick her up."

Megan hugged her two cousins, said goodbye to their husbands and watched them leave. She laid the half-eaten sandwich on her plate. "I want to go through the sailboat and check all its compartments."

"Do you expect to find a signed confession from the perpetrator?" Kyle asked in a sardonic voice.

"I don't know what I expect," she admitted. She shook her head in denial of her own words. "That's not true. I really don't expect to find anything, but I feel compelled to look in order to be sure there isn't."

He nodded. ''Actually, I feel the same.''

When he finished his lunch, she helped clean up the kitchen, then went with him to the boathouse. Carefully, they climbed aboard the yacht, testing each step as they went below. After a thorough search, they climbed back on the dock.

''Well, that's that,'' he said, his disgruntled gaze sweeping over the wreck.

She turned toward the dory tied at the end of the pier. ''I'd better go.''

''Stay.''

Stopped by the murmured request, she could only stare at him, awareness in every nerve of her body.

''Let's relax in the hot tub.''

His voice was quiet. Gentleness and longing mingled in the undercurrents that ran unseen between them.

She hadn't realized love could feel this way—so filled with hunger, yet so tender. Fierce, yet fragile. A million songs and poems had been written about love, yet she found it was impossible to speak of.

''If I stay...'' she began, then stopped. She knew what would happen. So did he.

Flames appeared in the depths of his eyes. ''Yes.''

His smile was rueful, expressing amusement at their shared dilemma of wanting each other and knowing it was unwise to give in to the wanting.

''We could be mortal enemies,'' she reminded him. ''If we ever find out the truth.''

''We could be...but we're not at the moment.''

When he held out a hand, she laid hers in it. Together they walked up the dock, away from the yacht and its secrets. At the hot tub, they undressed slowly, side by side, then, again holding hands, slipped into the frothy warmth together.

Time, Megan found, could simply disappear.

Kyle awoke and was immediately aware of the emptiness of his bed. He spotted Megan at the window, staring out into the night. She wore an old flannel shirt of his. For some reason, this fact made his heart dip.

This woman was the first he'd ever invited to *his* bed. He'd always preferred to be the one who could gracefully leave. He pulled on sweatpants and went to her. "Need a distraction?" he asked, keeping it light between them. She seemed incredibly fragile, as if her slender frame might vanish into a mist at his touch. Tenderness pulled at him.

She glanced up in question, but it was as if she saw beyond him to a place he couldn't go. Worry joined the web of emotion she induced in him.

"The insomnia cure," he reminded her.

"Oh. Oh, no. I mean..." She stopped, then smiled at him. "It's nearly dawn. I should go."

He found he didn't want her to. He ran his fingers through her hair, smoothing the tangles, liking the coolness of it, then the warmth next to her scalp. "I've never wanted to grab a woman up and run off with her before now. It's a caveman sort of thing, I suppose, but suddenly I understand the whole concept."

Although the sky steadily brightened, her eyes seemed to darken in the morning light. She laughed, but he sensed the sorrow that filled her heart. It reached right down and squeezed that sensitive place deep inside.

"Why so sad?" he asked.

"Loving someone can be so hopeless. The way my mother loved my father. The way my father was always trapped between his love for his wife and his father, and the ranch, which was his home. He once told me he felt part of the land. Sometimes fate plays cruel games with people."

"The way it has with us?"

She looked down and refused to answer. At last she sighed. "I really need to go."

"All right. I'll take you—"

"I have the dory," she quickly said.

He nodded. The sailboat had upset her more than he thought it would, considering they had already explored it pretty thoroughly when it was still in the water. He thought the hidden memories were bothering her, the ones she could only face in a nightmare, and wondered what they were.

Did he really want to know?

It was a question he didn't want to think about.

They dressed and went outside. A crisp breeze blew across the lake, bringing the cold mountain air down into the valley. The sun hadn't yet cleared the horizon above the eastern peaks.

There was loneliness to the world at this time of

day. He felt it clear to his soul—that, and the need to hold on to the woman who wanted to leave.

"I found my grandmother's journals," she said suddenly, her gaze on the house across the lake. "It was true about Grandfather needing money when he married. The ranch was having financial problems, it appears."

"Huh. Most ranches do."

"Apparently the rumor about Mary Dee's brother being in trouble with the law was true. Shannon found he'd been arrested for rustling, then cleared of all charges shortly after she married your grandfather. He must have settled things with the rancher whose cattle were stolen."

"I'd heard that gossip."

"We think our grandfather refused to help because he couldn't afford it. His pride probably wouldn't let him admit this to his future bride, so they quarreled and parted."

"So, one mystery solved at last," he said, his tone harsher than he meant it to be as he recalled the past.

"Well, resolved in our minds, at any rate."

She smiled again, but her eyes were dark. He steadied her with a hand on her arm as she stepped into the old fishing boat, then he shoved the bow away from the dock and watched as Megan guided the dory slowly, then faster, from him as she cleared the shallow waters and headed for the middle of the lake.

Eyes narrowed against the rising run, he watched her and the dory grow smaller. For some reason, he had a hunch she wasn't telling him everything. And that her thoughts were infinitely troubling.

A car engine jerked him out of his reverie. Turning, he was surprised to see his mother had arrived. He strode back to the house and took her large bag as she said goodbye to her friend.

"What are you doing home?" he asked.

"And a good morning to you, too," she said in a waspish tone. "I assume you haven't been watching the news. There was a heat wave in New York. The air conditioning at the hotel failed. We decided to come home."

"Sorry. I wasn't expecting you until next week."

"So I see." Her eyes followed the boat crossing the lake, then she studied him as if not sure he was her son.

He headed inside. "It's a long story," he said to her silent questioning. "Let's have breakfast."

When they were in the kitchen, he put on a pot of coffee while she got out a skillet, eggs and grated cheese for an omelet. "Are you seeing the Windom girl?"

"We've been working together on a project."

His mother broke the eggs, beat them and poured them into the skillet. She added a generous helping of cheese. "What kind of project?"

"We've brought up the sailboat."

She looked perplexed. "What sailboat?"

He tried to speak gently. "The one Dad went down in. I want to study it, then I'd like to restore it—"

"No," she said. "I don't want… Let it stay down there. Let the past stay buried."

"It's too late. Megan and I brought it up with her uncle's help. It's in the boathouse."

"Why?"

His mother had gone pale. Shock was rampant in her eyes. Guilt ate at him for reminding her of past hurts.

"Because I wanted to know if it would show us anything. I figured it's better to face things than bury them."

His mother turned off the burner and sank into a chair. "It was the wedding, wasn't it?" she said slowly. "I watched you dance with that girl…and I knew…I saw it in your eyes."

Kyle finished preparing the meal, divided the omelet between two plates and set them on the table. He poured them each a cup of coffee. His mother's hands shook as she raised the cup to her lips as if reaching for a lifeline. He was torn between his concern for her and the need to pursue the mystery. And yes, there were his feelings for Megan to be considered, too.

Was this how his father had felt when he took Bunny Windom on that sailing excursion that had been their last, moved by compassion for an unhappy woman…or torn by his love for her and loyalty to his family?

"I can't say there's nothing between us," he admitted. "There is."

"What…where will it lead?"

Pain hit him deep inside. "I don't know. Nowhere, I suppose. She's as skeptical as you are."

His mother closed her eyes, then gave him a look filled with sorrow and reproach. "You're in love with her."

He considered the hunger, the need, the sense of desolation when she left him. "We haven't discussed it," he said, forcing a lightness he was far from feeling.

Joan pressed a hand against her eyes. "Will it never end, this attraction between the Herriots and Windoms?"

He'd never heard her sound so discouraged. "Do you think there was something between Dad and Bunny Windom?"

"Haven't you heard—the wife is always the last to know?" she said wearily. She took another sip of coffee, then picked up her fork. "If there was, I never suspected it. A rancher stays pretty close to home. Jim never missed a meal that I remember."

"He always said you were the best cook in three counties." Kyle shook his head. "I'm tired of the questions. Surely there's some way to find the truth from the past. If Megan could but remember..."

"So you think she's the key?"

"Yes."

"The boat might make her remember?"

"I'd hoped so," he said, realizing that had been at the back of his mind, in case they didn't find real evidence. "I think she's the only living person who has a clue. She might have witnessed whatever happened."

"She was a child," Joan murmured. "She would have been frightened by a violent quarrel." She raised shocked eyes to his. "I never thought I'd say this, but maybe it's better for her not to have to recall that day."

"I wonder if she already has," he said, pondering on her distance from him that morning, on the almost desperate nature of her lovemaking during the night. "She could be keeping it from others. She wouldn't want to hurt her cousins. They're close."

"The Windom girls," Joan said, her face hardening slightly in spite of the sympathy. "They were always clannish."

Kyle thought of the tragedies the family had faced. "I guess they had to be. I think they had only each other to cling to most of their lives."

Joan rose and put her dishes in the dishwasher. "Every family has hard times," she said briskly, reverting to her usual no-nonsense approach to life.

"Megan the most of all," he said, feeling the sadness she'd tried to hide from her family yesterday and from him that morning.

"Whatever problems they've had, I'm sure they brought most of them down on their own heads. And on others." She picked up her purse. "I'm going to shower and try to sleep a while. I have a fierce headache."

Kyle sat at the table, his thoughts going from his mother, who hadn't forgiven the Windoms for their part in her husband's death, to Megan and her family and his strong conviction that her father had caused the latest tragedy between their families.

Megan knew it. He was more and more certain of that. Maybe she hadn't fully admitted it yet, but he thought that knowledge, hidden deep within her subconscious, was what was keeping her awake at night.

So where did that leave him and her?

No answer came to him. For the first time in his life, he didn't have a clear picture of the future. No good had ever come from an involvement between a Herriot and a Windom. It could only mean heartache for both sides. That much he knew.

Chapter Eleven

Megan stepped out of the shower, but she didn't feel refreshed. Monday was her hardest day, filled with riding classes that were exhausting in a different way from working only with animals.

Mothers.

One had actually shouted at her. The woman's daughter was afraid of horses and didn't want to take more lessons. Megan had suggested they find something more suitable for the girl. The mother had been furious.

She dried herself and slipped into pajamas and warm moccasins. After a bowl of canned soup, she watched the news, then restless, roamed the house. Without meaning to, she ended up in her grandfather's office.

Sitting at the massive roll-top desk, she pondered the information in the journals, the bits and pieces of memory she could muster and the terrifying uncertainty of her nightmares.

Following Shannon's advice, Megan had been telling herself to start at the beginning and follow the dream from start to finish. But somehow she couldn't.

Maybe she didn't know what had started the chain of events in her dreams. Perhaps she'd come in at the middle or at the end, seeing only the horrible finale. Or maybe she hadn't seen anything, and the dreams were the trauma of losing her mother as her father had said.

She pressed her hands over her eyes and felt the weariness reach all the way to her soul. She was tired of the nightmares and the uncertainty they represented in her life. She wanted to be finished with the past.

Because she wanted a future.

Like the dawn light brightening the horizon in shades of pink and gold and lavender, her love for Kyle asserted itself, growing stronger every moment she spent with him.

Her lover. Her enemy.

Except he didn't feel like an enemy. He was life and happiness, a richness of spirit she had never known existed. He made her want to sing and laugh and climb mountains.

Her images were a young girl's fancy, one whose

ideals hadn't been spoiled by life. She'd lost that girl a long time ago…when she'd been eleven….

The painful ache of longing settled over her. To have spent the night in Kyle's arms was foolish, but also utterly wonderful. Her lips trembled even as she smiled. Last night had been a sweet memory. She would add it to the sad ones, a silver lining to overlay the haunting grief she couldn't dispel or ignore.

Idly, she opened the middle drawer of the desk. She removed it completely and searched behind it, under it, checked for a secret compartment with an ice pick from the kitchen. Nothing.

She did the same with the other drawers as well as the back and sides and bottom. Finally she gave up, satisfied she had truly done her best. Eyeing the cubbyholes, she looked through them again, although most were now empty.

Pulling out the postcard from Mary Dee to her grandfather, she read it again and wondered why he'd kept it all these years. She read both sides and studied the ship's postmark, which was illegible. Then she noticed the date jotted in the upper left-hand corner.

The first day in June. The year had blurred—maybe a drop of water, or a tear, had fallen there—but Megan knew the year they were to have married.

Going to the wall safe, she pushed the picture aside and tried the new date. As easily as that, the tumblers clicked and the lock was freed.

She stared at it as if expecting a booby trap within, then she pulled the metal door open. Her heart beat slowly, heavily, drowning the night sounds through the open windows.

The vault was shallow, fitting easily between the wall studs. Inside she found a small jewelry box containing an engagement ring, wedding band and matching necklace belonging to Grandmother Rose. Megan had assumed her grandfather had sold those for cash years ago.

Beneath the velvet box was an envelope. She withdrew it, then, seeing there was nothing else, she retreated to the chair before opening it. She found it wasn't sealed.

Slipping the lined piece of notebook paper free, she carefully unfolded it. Her grandfather's writing covered the page. The letters were awkward and shaky, indicating he'd written it after his stroke.

Megan drew a deep breath and began to read.

When she'd finished, she closed her eyes. The terrible, terrible darkness beat at her, but she couldn't hear the ravens' wings. It was as if she'd gone deaf.

Memories, slowly, then faster, rushed at her from the dark closet of the past. She knew the truth, and it was truly awful....

The day had been much like any other June day. Her father had left early that morning with a load of cattle, heading for the auction down in Cheyenne.

Her mother had stayed late in bed that morning as she had all week. She'd lost a child a week ago. At eleven, Megan knew enough about birth and death to know what that meant. That morning, she'd heard her mother tell her father she wanted to leave the ranch, that she couldn't bear it. Sean had soothed his wife, saying she would feel better soon, then they would discuss it.

Megan had been quiet at breakfast, the way kids are when trouble is brewing in the family. She thought her grandfather knew of the talk between her parents. He'd been grim and silent during the meal that only the two of them had attended.

When the day warmed, she went outside. Her mother came down and sat on the patio and watched her play, but when Megan brought her ball and bat out, her mom had said she wasn't well enough to play. Megan had abandoned them on the patio and gone down toward the lake to climb her favorite tree. After hanging upside down for a while and watching the scene from that perspective, she went on up.

Once safe above the world on her little platform, she selected a book from the ones hidden in a waterproof backpack left hanging from a rusty nail she'd put up for this purpose.

Later, hearing an engine start, she saw her mother leave the dock in the little fishing boat and was angry at being left behind. No one wanted her that day. Her father had refused to let her accompany him, too.

Forgetting them, she became immersed in the story, then angry voices interrupted her idyll. Her mother stood on the dock beside Kyle Herriot's father while her grandfather yelled at them. She leaned forward to see better through the tree leaves.

Her eyes widened when she realized her mother

was crying. Mr. Herriot looked mad. "She ran out of gas," he said, gesturing toward her mother. Then, to her astonishment, her grandfather lifted his cane like a club, its heavy silver head shining in the sunlight. Mr. Herriot jumped aside and took a blow to the shoulder.

Grandfather hit him again, a sideways blow to the ribs that sent the other man reeling. Her mother screamed.

Turning and swinging the cane at the same time, her grandfather struck out again.

The scream stopped abruptly.

In the sudden silence, Megan heard the harsh caw of the ravens from the trees surrounding the gazebo. She strained to see what had happened.

The leaves shifted in the breeze. She saw her mother lying on the dock. Then she saw the blood. All over her mother's face.

She heard herself scream. Then she was falling. She remembered grabbing at branches, then the breath was knocked from her body as she hit the ground, flat on her back, her head smacking a flagstone on the path to the pier…

Megan pulled her hands down from her ears and clasped them in her lap. The fall was the last thing she recalled from the scene. She'd passed out when she hit the ground.

Later, when she came to, her father was lifting her from the floor of her closet. She'd started crying.

"Hush," he'd said. "It's okay. You'll be okay."

But she'd known even then that nothing would

ever be the same again. She tried to ask about her mother. "What...where..."

"You fell from the tree, probably got a slight concussion. You have to stay in bed."

She cried harder.

"Shh. You need to sleep. Just go to sleep. I'll stay by you. Go to sleep."

She had. It had been nearly dark when she'd awakened, her father's hand on her forehead. He sat on the bed and rubbed her forehead lightly. His hair had been wet, as if he'd just taken a shower.

When she heard the crows gathering to roost as night drew near, she'd cried out in terror. Her father had held her close. "It's just a dream," he said over and over. "It'll be all right. Sleep now. Sleep."

All her memories had vanished, of the past and of the two days that followed. She knew she'd stayed in bed. Twice she'd hidden in the closet. Her father had given her medicine, which had eased the throbbing, persistent headache and chased the dreams away. A sedative? Probably.

The morning of her mother's funeral was the first day she clearly recalled. It was as if her life had been a slate, wiped clean by the horror of that day.

Now she knew why.

She also knew why her father had started drinking. The grief he'd carried to his grave had been mixed with suspicion. From one particularly violent quarrel just before her father had died, she knew he had suspected his own father in the deaths of his wife and Jimmy Herriot.

For good reason.

Bunny had been unconscious, probably barely breathing so that her breath was undetectable after that blow to the head. Thinking they were both dead, her grandfather must have sunk the sailboat, returned to the house in the dory, and obliterated any evidence of Jimmy Herriot's presence.

Due to his unbridled temper, the older man had lived with unbearable guilt for the rest of his life, especially after his son hit a bridge abutment one snowy night, spun across the road and wrapped his vehicle around a tree. Patrick Windom had suffered a severe stroke two days later, during his son's funeral.

Standing, Megan realized every muscle in her body was trembling, as had once happened when she'd had the flu and run a very high temperature. She crept upstairs to bed, ill to her soul.

After turning out the light, she stared at the house across the lake. In one wing of the house, a light went out, then came back on before going out again.

She reached for the lamp, pulled back, reached out, then withdrew. To answer Kyle's signal was to invite him over. Tonight she was too spent, too vulnerable, to rest in his arms. Her own conscience wouldn't permit it, not without telling him what had happened. And then, he would surely hate her family when he learned the truth.

Docs hc have to know the truth? some part of her questioned. Nothing could ever make up to the Herriots for their loss. What difference can it possibly make now, except to hurt people all over again?

Because, another part grimly replied, Mrs. Herriot deserved to know her husband hadn't been cheating on her. An innocent bystander, he'd been caught up in other people's troubles and paid a high price for his compassion.

Grandfather and his terrible temper. What havoc it had caused in all their lives.

She crawled into bed. She wished she could pull the sheet over her head and sink once more into oblivion, waking in the morning with no memories at all, not even those of ardent kisses and tender caresses in which she'd found her greatest bliss.

Staring into the inky blackness, she knew she was going to have to tell them all—Kyle, his mother and her family. It was the only fair and honorable thing to do.

But it was going to be hard...so very hard....

Tuesday night, Megan set out coffee cups and wineglasses on the sideboard in the living room. The coffeepot was full and bottles of both red and white wine were available. The irony of the situation wasn't lost on her. Like the sleuth in an Agatha Christie novel, she'd called all the principals together for the denouement.

Kate and Jess arrived first. Megan gave them each a hug and indicated they were to help themselves to drinks.

"Are you okay?" Kate asked anxiously. "You sounded so serious on the phone."

"I'm fine." Megan summoned a smile, but the fateful moment weighed heavily on her as they waited for the others to arrive.

Shannon and Rory were next. Kyle and his mother were last. Megan noted they arrived in a car rather than in the powerboat. She gravely welcomed them.

When everyone was seated, all eyes turned to her. She stood at the empty fireplace, her hands tucked into her folded arms to hide their trembling.

"I remember," she began, then stopped as her voice quavered ever so little. She swallowed and started over. "I remember most of the past now, I think."

"When?" Shannon asked, looking extremely worried.

"Yesterday." Megan glanced at the envelope on the mantel. When she looked back at the little group she'd called together, her eyes met Kyle's.

He looked from the paper to her. His expression was solemn, his thoughts carefully hidden. Her world shifted as a small rip opened in her soul. He would hate her....

"I thought it only fair that all of you should know the truth, or at least as much as I know of it." She inhaled slowly, carefully. "My nightmares were composed of snatches of various events, it seems."

"Start from your earliest memory," Shannon suggested, her tone firm and supportive, "and work through to the end. Please, don't anyone interrupt," she cautioned. She took a pen and notebook from her purse. "Okay."

"My mother had a miscarriage a week before the accident." Megan realized that wasn't the correct word. "Before the boating incident."

Joan Herriot gasped. Her fair complexion seemed to pale even more.

"There was never anything between Mr. Herriot and my mother. But there were bad feelings between her and my grandfather. He wanted a male heir. She'd had at least two miscarriages that I know of. He said she wasn't woman enough to give her husband a son. It made my father furious. I remember, the day before that last morning, hearing my mother weep and my father shout at Grandfather. My parents decided to leave the ranch. I found that very scary."

"Wait," Rory said. He left the room and returned with a dining-room chair for Megan.

Giving him a grateful smile, she took a seat and continued. "The next morning my father drove the cattle to the auction. My mother had avoided my grandfather, but when she came down to the patio, he came out, too. I was up in the tree by the path to the lake. That's when Grandfather said she was an evil woman who was driving her husband to leave the land he loved."

Kate shook her head, her expression sad but not surprised. Being the oldest of the grandchildren, she knew well what Patrick Windom had been like.

"Mother ran down to the dock and cast off in the dory. I remember being hurt because no one wanted me with them that day. My father had refused to take me to the auction earlier that morning.''

Clenching her hands in her lap, she told them the rest—her mother had run out of gas and Mr. Herriot had brought her home, her grandfather had shouted at them....

''It was my grandfather,'' she said directly to Kyle. ''He hit your father in the ribs, then he hit my mother on the head. I remember the sudden silence, then the crows started a racket over by the gazebo. I think that's why I dream of them, that they're attacking...''

''Grandfather and his temper,'' Kate murmured.

When Megan risked a glance at Kyle, he looked as if he'd been cast in granite, he sat so still. His mother was clearly horrified.

''So your grandfather sailed the boat to the rocks and scuttled it,'' Kyle concluded.

Megan nodded. ''This is speculation on my part. I fell from the tree and hit my head on a flagstone, I think. I somehow made it to my room and passed out. Then my father was there. He put me in bed and told me to sleep. Then he went away. I assume he'd sold the cattle before the auction and come home early.''

Shannon looked up from her notes. ''You shouldn't have been left alone. You might have had a concussion.''

''I'm pretty sure I did. My head hurt for several days. I think I was given sedatives of some kind.''

''That was dangerous,'' Shannon interrupted.

Megan gave her cousin a rueful smile. ''Father did the best he could at the time. He was the one who reported my mother missing and helped with the exploration of the lake. After the autopsy, he found out my mother hadn't been dead when the yacht went down. He blamed himself. He said if he'd been home he could have prevented the accident.''

''Poor Uncle Sean. No wonder he drank himself to death.''

Megan nodded at Kate. ''He was so unhappy after Mother's death. At times he seemed to hate Grandfather, at others, himself. By then, I think he'd begun to doubt my grandfather's version of the day's events.''

''With reason,'' Kyle said, his voice and eyes as cold as glacier ice. ''If the man had had any spine at all, he would have come forward with his suspicions.''

''He couldn't.'' Shannon at once defended her relative. ''He couldn't send his own father to jail.''

''It would have been useless in any case. He had no proof,'' Jess informed them.

Megan shivered. ''When he got the police report, he knew Mother had drowned when the boat went down. It must have been horrible for him—'' Her throat closed.

Mrs. Herriot rose suddenly. Her lips were ashen, but her neck was mottled with splotches of red. She refused to look at any of the cousins, but Megan felt the woman's hatred as a palpable thing. She couldn't blame her for it.

"I want to go home," she said to her son. "Take me home. Now."

"I'm terribly sorry, Mrs. Herriot," Megan said. "If it's any comfort, I know my grandfather didn't mean to seriously injure anyone. I saw his face when he realized the other two weren't moving. He was horrified."

Kyle's gaze swept over the three cousins, paused at her, then moved on, but not before she'd seen the darkness reaching all the way to his soul. He took his mother's arm and guided her toward the door.

Long after the sound of their car engine faded into the night, Megan felt the finality of that last glance. At last, she spoke. "What do we do now?" she asked, looking at her uncle.

"Tell the sheriff," Jess replied.

"I suppose we have to."

He nodded. "The case should be laid to rest. I'll need the letter from your grandfather for the file."

Megan handed it over. Jess, then the others, read it and shook their heads in pity, regret and other emotions too tangled to sort out.

She and the two couples talked until eleven, then Kate and Jess had to go home to relieve their babysitter. Shannon and Rory stayed.

"Come home with us," Shannon urged. "I don't want you to be alone."

Megan shook her head. "I'm all right. Really. I understand the nightmares now. That's a relief, to tell the truth. Everything has fallen into place."

"How could Grandfather have been so foolish?" Shannon questioned sadly.

"He was tortured for it," Rory assured his wife, touching her gently on the shoulder, "for the rest of his life."

"Yes, but so were Megan and Uncle Sean."

"And Mrs. Herriot and Kyle," Megan added. "Mr. Herriot was truly an innocent bystander who happened to be at the wrong place at the wrong time. I feel so guilty about that. I know now he was simply trying to help. If only I could have remembered sooner. But I didn't."

Shannon stood with a sigh. "We should go. I wish you'd come home with us. Or do you want me to stay here?"

"I've accepted what happened," Megan said, managing a smile of sorts, which was probably as sad as Shannon's eyes. "And guess what? No bad dreams last night," she added on a forced note of cheer.

Shannon hugged her tight. "Call if you need me, no matter what time of the day or night, even if you just want someone to cry with. Okay?"

"I will. I promise."

Megan walked them to their car and saw them off. After their taillights disappeared, she stood on the patio and gazed at the night scene, her mind and emotions curiously blank. As if she'd given her all to some mighty battle and had nothing left inside.

Across the lake, she saw several lights on in different rooms. Neither Kyle nor his mother was asleep. There would be little rest for any of them that night.

Going inside, she realized that while they now knew the sequence of events on that terrible day, the who and what and why of it, so that they had closure, none of them could ever escape completely from the past.

In her own heart, she found it hard to forgive her grandfather for his actions or for his cowardice in not telling the truth. If he'd called for help immediately, then her mother might have survived the blow. They could have found a new life as a family....

Well, it would be nice to think so, but maybe not. Maybe their fates had been sealed long before the actual event, maybe from the moment Sean Windom fell in love with a pretty waitress trying to work her way through college and make a better life for herself.

Who could say?

Megan sat in the dark, legs crossed, on the end of the bed. It was now past midnight.

The lights had gone out in the Herriot household, except for the outside ones concealed in the shrubbery. She wondered what Kyle was doing and if he'd managed to go to sleep. She wondered if he hated her and her family.

On an impulse, she flicked the bedside lamp on, then turned it off. Her heart pounded so hard she actually felt it hurt with each beat as she waited to see what would happen next.

To her shock, a light went on, then off, across the lake. In a few minutes she heard the low drone of an engine approaching her dock.

Heart racing, she ran downstairs, turned on the patio and pier lights, then opened the door.

The cold mountain air penetrated her pajamas as she watched a lone male figure tie up, then walk across the lawn. He stopped at the open door.

They looked at each other in the dim light of a half moon. Neither smiled or spoke for a long minute. When she stepped back, he came inside and closed the door behind him.

"You came," she said, not quite able to believe it.

"Yes." He took her face between his hands and gazed deeply into her eyes. "Even now, even knowing…I still can't resist you."

His short laugh was filled with irony and resignation. It hurt in that secret place. She hung her head. "Then go."

"I can't," he admitted.

"Then stay and be damned to whatever fates there are," she whispered fiercely and dived into his arms.

He held her so close she could hardly breathe. Air didn't seem necessary. His embrace did. She held him just as tightly. Long minutes ticked by.

They turned and, arm in arm, walked up the broad steps and into the magic of moonlight and mist.

In her room, in bed, they exchanged a thousand caresses, a thousand sighs. Demand met longing and for the moment both were appeased.

They stayed together until the dawn, not sleeping, not speaking, communicating only by touch. For Megan it was enough and yet not enough.

She knew what the morning would bring.

"I have to go," he said at last, as the early light that hinted at the coming dawn silhouetted the mountains.

"I know." She rose when he did and slipped into warm sweats as he dressed. "Do you want breakfast?"

"No."

"Coffee?" She grasped at the last precious moments, knowing she could never quite hold on to them.

He shook his head.

At the door, he stopped and gazed at her a long time, as if he would memorize each nuance of the moment. His eyes, so beautiful, so sad, made her want to weep.

Reaching out, she stroked once down his lean cheek, then let her hand fall to her side. Nothing could ever work between them. The past had been too harsh. There was no point in prolonging the moment.

She finally spoke. "It was foolish to signal you. I won't do it again. It's no good, our seeing each other."

He frowned. "So that's it?" he questioned. "All this for nothing?" He gestured between them as if drawing attention to some fragile but elemental truth.

Longing rushed through her. For the time between

two heartbeats, she was weakened by it, but reality couldn't be denied. ''There's no future for us,'' she said doggedly, knowing love could never survive the hatred from the past.

Something like anger or agony, perhaps both, flashed through his eyes and was gone. ''I see.'' He looked utterly weary.

She bid him goodbye. Without a tear. Without a plea for forgiveness. He hesitated, then walked off and was enveloped by the fog covering the lake. Long after he was gone, she stood there on the patio, unable to think or move.

From beneath the old oak beside the path, she saw a figure emerge. A young girl stepped forward, her eyes as green as a mossy pool and so very solemn. She nodded once, then she, too, disappeared, a mist that faded in the dawn.

''Goodbye,'' Megan whispered to that child. ''Sweet dreams to you, forever and ever.''

The wind moaned through the cottonwoods, murmuring of days gone by and of those yet to come. Entering the empty house, she felt its loneliness wrap around her heart.

Chapter Twelve

Megan slipped into a chair at the diner. Saturdays were busy days in the small ranching community and normally she wouldn't have gone anywhere near town, but Kate had called and asked her to join the cousins for lunch.

Since she didn't have a class until two, she'd agreed, knowing Kate and Shannon would worry if she refused. They already thought she was becoming a recluse.

"I feel as if I've grown two heads," she murmured, spreading a napkin over her lap.

Shannon nodded in understanding. "Now that the report has come out in the newspaper, everyone knows."

"They're also adding to the story," Kate said. "Whether they know anything or not."

"It's human nature," Shannon concluded. She leaned forward and studied Megan. "How are you doing?"

"Fine. The nightmares seem to have truly gone."

"That's good. I'd hoped having everything resolved in your own mind would be the key."

The past was resolved, but not her love for a man who must hate all she stood for. "So what's happening with you two?" she asked after they'd given their orders to the waitress.

"Ah," Shannon said in a pleased voice. "Guess what?"

"What?" Megan and Kate asked together.

"My peripheral vision is good enough that I can drive again. As long as I wear glasses."

She wrinkled her nose, then laughed with the carefree abandon Megan remembered from their younger days. She and Kate laughed in joy, too. As she did, Megan was overwhelmed with other, deeper emotions.

The three cousins shared an enduring friendship, genuinely liking each other. They had each lived through tragedy and made it. Kate's first husband had wounded her and then killed himself. Shannon, a local cop, had been temporarily blinded by a shot in the head. She'd nearly died, but Rory had found her in time.

Now her two favorite people had found happiness with their new loves. With Jess, Kate had the family she'd always wanted. Shannon had her sight and a brand-new husband. A surge of fierce protective love rose in Megan. She wanted so much for them—happiness and contentment and all the good things in life.

"So now you're Dead-eye Dick again?" she teased, referring to the fact that Shannon had been an expert with her pistol at the police range.

"Almost. My left eye will always have a fuzzy spot where the nerve was damaged, but the right eye compensates for it. I normally don't even notice the difference."

"That's really great," Kate said. "I have some news, too. Jeremy's mother has dropped her custody suit. Jeremy apparently told her attorney he'd rather live with his father and visit his mom during the holidays."

Shannon nodded wisely. "At Jeremy's age, that would weigh heavily with the judge."

Kate nodded, then said, "But you know, I feel kind of sorry for his mother. I mean, she must feel rejected."

"You softie," Shannon accused.

"I'm glad Jeremy's going to live here," Megan told her cousin. "He's a wonderful helper. I really miss him."

She wished she hadn't added the last. Both cousins studied her, concern in their eyes. The waitress brought their plates before they could question her about her emotional state. She breathed a sigh of relief.

"Ah, my favorite three people," a male voice said.

Megan smiled as Rory gave Shannon a quick kiss on the cheek, then said hello to her and Kate.

"We have an extra chair," Shannon said. "Are you going to join us?"

"I wouldn't think of it. Kyle stopped by the office. He's in town today, so we're going to chow down." He eyed Megan. "The gossip is flying. You holding up okay?"

She ignored the frantic beating of her heart at the mention of Kyle. "Yes. It's no more than I expected. I've been stopped on the street at least a dozen times this morning. Everyone wants to tell me their impression of the story and what they thought at the time."

At that moment, the café door swung open and Kyle entered. There was a momentary lull in the conversation as the locals looked from him to her, then frankly watched to see what would happen.

Kyle came over. "Hello, ladies. Lovely day, isn't it?"

His voice combined just the right amount of wry humor and friendliness to reassure the avid diners that he held no rancor toward the Windom girls because of the past.

Megan knew better. His smile was friendly enough as he looked at Kate and Shannon. It disappeared when he turned her way. His glance, as it slid past her, was without a hint of warmth or amusement.

She didn't blame him for hating her, but it hurt. In an effort at control, she sipped some water, then found it was almost impossible to swallow. Her throat ached as she forced the liquid past the lump of misery that had settled there and waited desperately for the men to leave.

And through it all, she smiled and smiled and smiled.

"We can make room for you," Shannon said, her jaw set in its stubborn mode. "We only need one more chair."

Megan felt as if an abyss was opening right down the middle of her heart as another chair was pulled up. She shifted toward Kate while Rory naturally settled next to Shannon. That left Kyle to slide his chair in next to hers.

Electricity flashed along her nerves as her entire body went on red alert. She willed her hand not to tremble when she picked up her fork.

As the conversation continued around her, Megan sought and found the inner well of reserve she'd discovered long ago. She really hadn't expected to become immune to Kyle's presence in four days.

Right. She'd give it a week.

Her attempt at humor only caused the ache to grow.

"How's it going with the sailboat?" Rory asked. "You done any work on her?"

Kyle nodded. "I've repaired the hole and removed all the paneling and upholstered items. The inside is washed down with bleach. With the current heat wave, the hull is drying pretty fast."

"How's your mother doing?" Kate said. "What does she think about your having the boat?"

Megan couldn't look away as his mouth curved into a rueful smile. "She accepts that I was determined to find out all I could. I think she feels better knowing her husband wasn't involved with another woman. That rumor hurt more than she admitted. Thank you for sharing the truth," he said with grave sincerity to Megan, looking at her for the first time since he'd sat down.

His perusal stirred longing and unrest in her. Her heart raced. Noting the lack of expression in his silver-gray eyes, she looked away and shrugged. "I had to. It was only right."

But sometimes "right" could be very depressing she'd found during the wee hours of the night when sleep eluded her. She no longer had nightmares, but she dreamed of him and the fiery caresses they had shared. In the darkness of night, the loneliness reached all the way to her soul.

She ate, but her appetite had fled. It didn't take much to fill her up these days.

"You've lost weight," Kyle commented in an aside to her while the others discussed the terrible heat of the last few days and the increased danger of wildfire.

"It's the weather. I can't stand to cook. Not that I do much of that at any time," she added candidly.

When he smiled, her heart melted right down to her toes. She averted her eyes from his handsome face and quickly ate every bite on the plate. "I really have to go. Afternoon classes start at two."

"Lunch is on me," Rory declared when she pulled out her wallet.

"I'll split it with you," Kyle said firmly.

She hesitated, then decided not to argue. "Thanks, both of you. Have a super day," she said brightly, then hurried out. She was aware of Kyle's eyes on her all the way to her car, which was parked at the curb.

Once on the ranch road, she sighed and slowed down. She was running from her own emotions, she admitted. No demons chased after her the way the crows used to in the fragmented nightmares. It was only the future she had to worry about.

The future. She could see herself alone on the ranch, growing more eccentric with each passing year. Well, there were worse things to be. A liar. Or a murderer. She frowned. No good came from thinking about that.

She'd done her best to make reparations for past harm, she assured the part of her that still felt the weight of guilt over that. Kyle and his mother might never forgive her family, but that was something they would have to resolve for themselves.

At the house, she changed clothes, then went outside. The light wouldn't come on in the tack room. She flicked it impatiently. Finally it came on. She made a mental note to check out the sockets in the stable and grabbed a saddle.

Waiting for the riding class to assemble, she stroked the mane of her favorite mare. Today was the first day of July. A new month. Half a year gone by.

Handing out reminder notices for fees to parents, she saw herself as a little old lady, still training horses and teaching, only it was the children of the children she now taught who made up her classes. She sighed at the absurdity of it all—of longing and need and hunger, the whole crazy notion of falling in love.

When all the children were mounted, she swung up on the mare. "Today we're going to learn the proper way to jump. The rider sets the pace, then *lifts* the horse over the obstacle. If you're off, your mount will be off."

She demonstrated the technique. For the next fifty minutes she lost herself in the task of turning ten youngsters into accomplished riders, then she supervised the storing of tack and brushing down of the horses. At three-thirty, she worked with the cranky gelding for an hour.

Finished with all the chores shortly after six, she took a shower and changed to a knit outfit. Munching on a sandwich, she entered the monthly payments in the books. By eight-thirty, she was caught up on everything.

With nothing else to occupy her mind, she sat on the patio swing and pushed herself gently to and fro while evening shadows spread across the valley. For a while, she watched ripples roll across the lake, then she stared at the house across the way.

Always a busy person, she'd never realized what

loneliness was until Kyle had come, ever so briefly, into her life. Four weeks ago she'd danced with him, her enemy, for the first time. She'd found a different person that night—a man who was observant, one who could be kind, as he'd been when she'd gotten teary-eyed over Rory's concern for his bride.

In that short space of time, they'd become partners in raising the yacht, then lovers. They'd found the truth they were looking for. And now they were enemies again.

Full circle.

The odd melancholy settled over her spirits as the twilight settled over the land. It felt strangely gentle, but sad, and filled with yearning for things she couldn't quite name.

The colors of sunset gleamed upon the still surface of the lake, turning it into a surreal canvas of molten gold, silver and ebony. Out of the fiery glow, a single figure in a canoe emerged.

Kyle glided silently up to the dock. Across the wide lawn, his eyes met hers. With a gesture of one hand, he invited her to join him.

Without thinking, she rose and went to him. A single joy pulsed through her heart, that of being with him.

She pushed the canoe away from the dock and took the front seat. She paddled in leisurely strokes while he did the same. They left the broad middle of the lake and headed toward the narrows, where the way grew treacherous among hidden rocks and snags.

She guided them through the dangerous waters to the base of the granite cliff where once a glacier had nestled.

Snow lingered in a groove of rock high above them, and a creek ran from it to the lake, forming waterfalls like fairy veils along the cliff face. The two humans, small and frail in their tiny craft, skimmed along the talus base, a moving shadow among the deeper shadows there.

Following the shoreline, they came again into the last long fingers of light from the setting sun. The bow of the canoe turned before they reached her house, though. Kyle guided them into the shallow alcove where the gazebo stood in lonely splendor against the twilight.

A strand of rock provided a landing spot. She climbed out while he steadied the canoe, then he climbed out while she tied a line to a ring set in the stone. Together, but without touching, they walked over to the structure.

"My grandfather built this for my grandmother," she said when they reached the steps to the summer house. "She used to come here and read in the afternoons."

"Did you know her?"

"Not really. I was hardly more than a baby when she died. My mother said Grandfather never got over missing her. I think, in the end, he realized how much he loved her."

Megan sat on the top step and rested her head against a post. Kyle sat beside her. After a minute, he dropped an arm around her shoulders. She looked at him, a question in her eyes, and sensed the hunger between them.

"I don't know," he said. "Whatever you're asking, I don't know the answer."

She surprised them both by smiling. "I don't even know the question," she admitted, keeping her tone light.

He sighed, then gave a snort of laughter. "It's a whole new mystery in itself."

She thought they understood passion quite well, but she asked anyway. "What is?"

"Us. I guess that's the question. What do we do about us?"

"There is no us."

Sadness entered his eyes. "True."

She wished he hadn't agreed so readily.

"But," he continued, "there is this."

He hooked a finger under her chin and lifted her face to his. She came willingly. The kiss was unbearably tender. It brought the sting of tears to her eyes.

When he let her go, she shook her head. "It's crazy to prolong something that's useless."

"Tell that to the dreams that wake me at night, leaving me so restless I can't sleep."

His voice was weary, as if he'd fought this battle and lost many times. Despair burned in his eyes. But there was hunger, too. And need that was more than physical.

She wondered why solving the mystery of the past

hadn't solved the problems it had created between them.

Because, out of their own troubles, the Windoms had caused a tragedy for others. She hated that he'd been hurt as a boy, his family life destroyed due to an innocent act of compassion, that of helping a grieving neighbor home.

Wrapping her arms around Kyle, she tried to tell him through her touch how very sorry she was. She kissed his jaw, his cheek, the corner of his mouth where she felt a muscle clench against her lips.

"No," he said, pulling away and standing. "You're right. It's crazy to want like this, to give in to passion that has no place in either of our lives."

"I know." But for a minute she had hoped. She realized how futile it had been when she perused his closed face. He could never come to her without the specter of the past between them. She understood that perfectly. She'd lived with the ghost of her youthful self for fifteen years.

He gestured toward the canoe. "I'll take you home."

"It isn't far. I'd rather walk." She turned and strode up the path through the trees.

Rustling in the branches above her drew her attention to roosting birds and their displeasure at the human intrusion. She spotted a crow watching her with its unblinking stare. A shiver chased down her arms.

Hurrying now, she jogged across the pasture and up to the patio. On the lake she could barely make out a lone canoe gliding silently along its surface.

For a moment, it and the man seemed surreal, a fragment left from long ago, from a time when she'd thought life would be filled with sunshine everyday.

She rushed into the house and locked the dead bolt behind her as if it could shut out the memory of grief and unhappiness and a love she could never claim.

Kyle heard his mother's car when she returned home from church, but he didn't pause in the methodical sanding of the yacht railing. He'd spent every moment he could spare from ranch business—and some he couldn't—working on the sailboat.

Sweat ran down his face and chest, soaking into the old ragged cutoffs he wore. July had been one of the hottest months on record, and the driest. Forest fires burned in several places across the state. Fortunately none of them was in this valley.

Restoring the boat, he'd found, occupied his mind enough that he didn't dwell on other things, such as what was happening across the lake. He continued with the task.

"I can't believe you've accomplished so much in a month," his mother said, startling him, since he hadn't heard her approach along the dock.

He saw she'd changed to a casual outfit of blue knit that exactly matched the blue in her eyes. Then, for the oddest moment in the still water under the boat slip, he saw eyes of mossy green outlined in charcoal gray. He shook his head slightly and the vision was gone.

"This section of railing is the last," he said. "As

soon as I finish sanding and get it varnished, I'll put the new sails on and take her for a trial run.''

She nodded and came inside, taking a seat on the plastic lawn chair where he sometimes ate a sandwich and scrutinized his work on the yacht.

''Your father loved working on this boat,'' she said in a musing tone. Her smile was nostalgic. ''So did your grandfather. He saw it beside a barn next to the highway down near Cheyenne, going to ruin. He bought it and fixed it up himself. He'd never even sailed, but he taught himself here on the lake. Do you remember the Sunday picnics we used to have on it?''

''Yes.'' He finished the last round of sanding and stepped back to admire the wood grain in the railing.

''Your grandmother loved those. I thought they were fun, too. As a boy, you couldn't decide between that and ice skating on the lake in winter as the very best thing.''

''I remember.'' The weight of the past pressed on him, reminding him of old hurts. His twelfth birthday had occurred right after the boating incident. The planned birthday party had been canceled. He had both resented that fact and felt guilty for the resentment.

Funny, but he couldn't even remember what his mother or grandmother had gotten him for a present. The days after the sinking of the yacht had run together like a movie in fast forward. He hadn't been able to understand all that was happening at the time.

He thought of Megan's amnesia and hardened his

heart against pity. She'd been a child, but if she could have recalled the terrible day, she could have saved them all years of uncertainty—

His mother went on. "You were always so eager to try new things. I worried about your adventuresome spirit, but your father and grandfather encouraged you."

Kyle grinned when she gave him a playful grimace. She'd changed, he realized. That month, she'd brought up the past several times, only happy incidents, true, but still she seemed…more at ease about it. He was glad for her.

Using an old T-shirt, he wiped moisture and sawdust off his face and down the front of his torso before pulling another lawn chair up and taking a seat. He wished he could find some kind of peace within himself.

"When do you think the *Mary Dee* will be ready to take out for the test run?" his mom asked.

"It'll probably be another week, maybe two. I have to varnish the deck railing first."

"I'm surprised the Windom girl…Megan…isn't helping. The boat *is* half hers, isn't it?"

The question took him by surprise—no, more like an ambush. A hot spear of need shot through him with lightning speed, setting off fires within that couldn't easily be quenched. It happened every time there was any kind of reference to her, or anything that forced him to acknowledge her existence a quarter mile away, with only the lake between. He'd found it easier not to think of her at all.

"I'm going to buy her out," he said, his tone dropping into a husky register which he hoped didn't reveal the turmoil within.

"Oh."

He was relieved when she didn't pursue the subject, but stood as if going back to the house. "I'll fix lunch. Shall I bring it down here?"

"Uh, that's okay. I'll come up to the house in about half an hour. I'll clean up the sawdust first, then tomorrow I can start varnishing."

"We'll eat on the patio," she decided. "Then I want to talk to you about an idea Marge and I had."

After she went up to the house, he vacuumed up the sawdust, then wiped the railings down with a cloth. The wood was smooth as butter to the touch.

As smooth as a woman's skin.

The thought came unbidden and with it, images of the hours he'd spent with Megan in her bed, in his, in hers again. Those brief interludes didn't constitute an affair.

But they'd been enough to fill his nights with restless dreams and wakeful hours of hunger.

He cursed, but it didn't drive the visions from his head, nor the tension from his body. Fury and passion pounded through him in equal parts. Logic said Megan was right; there was no future for them. Seeing him would be a constant reminder of the traumatic scene she'd witnessed.

It was a "damned if you do, damned if you don't" situation. Gritting his teeth, he ignored the raging hunger of his body, finished cleaning up, then jogged up to the house to shower and change for lunch.

After they'd eaten, he rose to take his dishes to the kitchen, but his mother held up a hand. "Wait. I want to run an idea by you."

He settled back into the chair and tried not to gaze at the house across the lake. He'd seen no activity at all over there that morning. Megan was probably visiting with one of her cousins.

"Marge and I are thinking of going in together and buying a condo on the Gulf coast of Alabama."

She may as well have said the two widows and lifelong friends were thinking of starting a honky-tonk for all the sense her words made.

"What?"

She laughed. He was surprised at how young and delighted she sounded. And looked. She appeared young and pretty all at once. His mother, he realized, wasn't all that old by today's standards.

"The winters are harsh up here," she continued. "I'd like a warmer climate. Your father and I honeymooned at Gulf Shores, you know. It has good memories for me."

He didn't recall whether he'd known that or not.

"What do you think? Would you mind being alone most of the year? We plan to spend the summers here in the mountains, and thus have the best of both worlds."

"I think that sounds like a great idea," he agreed, studying his mother surreptitiously, trying to figure out what was different.

"So do I. As Marge said, perhaps it's time we made a change in our lives." She gazed toward the boathouse. "To put the past truly behind us and make a new life."

"Is that what you're going to do?"

"I hope so. I truly hope so," she repeated, giving him a keen glance. "You should think about your future, too. It's time you found a wife and started your family. I want grandchildren. Marge has three. I feel left out."

At her laughter—almost a girlish giggle—he chuckled, too. "Give me time," he pleaded his case. "I'm not even thirty yet."

His mother became serious. "Don't throw away years in useless grief the way I did," she advised. "Let it go. I want you to find a wonderful love and fill your days with happiness."

"We can only wish," he said sardonically, humoring her. "Maybe I'll meet *the* woman on my next trip to town."

She glanced at him, then across the lake. "I think you've already met her," she said, her gaze going soft, a sadness in the clear blue depths.

Before he could think of a denial, she rose, gathered the dishes and went inside. He continued to sit on the deck, its silvery-gray planks shaded by an oak tree his father had planted the year he was born. He thought of the other children they had wanted to have. He, too, had wanted a brother or sister.

A longing rose in him, for something he couldn't

identify, yet he knew he wanted that elusive thing, whatever it was, very, very much.

A wife?

A family of his own?

It wasn't something he'd consciously thought of. He'd always assumed he'd know it immediately when he met the right woman. Right. Just like Romeo and Juliet, love at first sight.

He didn't think a fairy-tale love was in the cards for him. Not yet at any rate.

From across the way, he saw the old station wagon that Megan drove stir up a lazy swirl of dust as she arrived home. In a few minutes he saw her, in jeans and shirt, heading for the stable to tend the ever-necessary chores of a ranch.

Something in him clenched painfully. If things had been different, maybe…maybe…

He didn't complete the useless thought. Rising, he headed for the boathouse and the work that consumed him there.

Chapter Thirteen

Megan entered the darkness of the stable. The day was another scorcher and any respite from the sun was a relief. With stored hay providing insulation in the loft, the stable stayed several degrees cooler than the great outdoors.

She flicked on the light switch. Nothing happened. She flicked it again. The two overhead lights came on.

Darn, she'd forgotten to check the lights and wiring. No time now. She went into the first stall to check the mare. Last night she'd thought the animal was limping a bit and had brought her in for a liniment rubdown.

Leading the mare and letting her frisky baby tag along, Megan went into the corral adjoining the stable and walked her for a few minutes. The mare still had a slight limp.

Frowning, Megan ran a hand down the leg, but found nothing wrong. She'd have Rory take a look at it.

Going inside for a bucket of feed, she paused and sniffed the air. For a second, she'd thought she'd smelled smoke, but she didn't detect any now. She measured feed for the mare and set the bucket in the corral.

After feeding and watering the boarded stock, she turned most of them out in the pasture, except for the ones she was training. Going back into the stable, she again caught a whiff of smoke. Worried now, she checked each tack and storage room, but found nothing.

Suddenly, above her, she heard a roaring sound, like an explosion without the first loud *crack* that sets it off. She knew immediately what it was. The hay had caught fire!

Grabbing the fire extinguisher, she raced up the ladder. Flames billowed over her as soon as she threw open the trapdoor to the loft. Ducking down, she directed a stream of spray directly at them. A draft started, drawing the smoke and fire upward as air rushed into the opening.

Megan risked a glance into the loft. An inferno of leaping, roaring flames greeted her.

Leaping off the ladder, she landed with a thud and opened the stalls of the four training horses. "Git. Git," she shouted at the animals. As soon as they stampeded for the door, she headed for the house. In the kitchen, she dialed 911 and tersely told the dispatcher, "Fire at the Windom ranch. The stable is burning. Send the fire department."

"Right. Please stay on the line."

"The county fire department," she said again. "Tell them to hurry."

In the corral next to the stable, the mare ran in a frenzied line up and down the rail fence. Megan realized she had to get her and the filly moved away from the intense heat.

"Hello? Hello?" she said, but got no answer from the dispatcher. "I've got to go down to the corral," she said into the phone. "I have to move the mare."

Dropping the phone on the counter, she dashed outside. She heard the mare whickering in alarm, but another horse was screaming in panic. Puzzled, she stopped and peered into the open door of the stable.

Black smoke and flames engulfed the lower part now. The roof was only a skeleton of rafters with flames shooting skyward between them.

She heard another scream, then saw the outline of a horse against the flames. One of the horses was still inside! Looking toward the frightened mare and filly, she realized she had to move them. The wooden railing was on fire and the stable might collapse in that direction when it crumbled. She leaped over the rails and opened the gate to the pasture.

"Hi-yah," she yelled, waving her arms.

The mare, eyes rolling, ran by her and out into the pasture, the long-legged filly at her heels.

Megan set to the task of saving the surly gelding. Turning on the hose full-force, she advanced into the fire, its roar of fury like that of a derailing locomotive. If she could get behind the gelding, she could drive him out and wet him down at the same time.

Pushing the leaping tongues of fire back with the hose, she advanced inside. The gelding plunged and kicked at the flames, screaming in fear and fury. She got between him and the door, then turned the stream of water on him and the flaming post behind him.

''Hi-yah,'' she yelled. ''Get out of here.''

The gelding turned on her. He reared, front hooves striking out. Surprised, she raised her arms and ducked at the same time. The water hit the gelding in the face.

Enraged and out of control, he lunged at her, his shoulder catching her in the chest.

Megan stumbled backward. Her head struck the corner post of a stall. Her vision narrowed like a lens with dust gathering at the edges, then went dark. Desperately she held on to the hose and felt its spray rain down on her. The gelding backed away.

''Git,'' she yelled. ''Git out of here, you mangy—''

A rafter fell to the floor between them. With another scream, the gelding spun and raced out of the stable and across the lawn, nearly running over the man who raced up the slope from the lake.

Kyle dodged the spooked horse and headed for the stable at a dead run. Megan was in there!

Inside, he had to stop at the wall of flames produced by a burning rafter. The stalls and wooden walls were also engulfed in flames.

Beyond the rafter, Megan struggled to her feet. Looking dazed, she turned the hose on the flames, then she spotted him. "Stay back," she called. "The roof is going."

"Come out of there," he yelled.

"Can't. Got to check the stalls...to be sure..." She put a hand to her head, then looked at her fingers, which came away bloody. "I hit my head," she explained to him over the racket of the inferno.

Gritting his teeth, he took a running jump and leaped over the rafter. Grabbing Megan, he took the hose away from her and cleared a spot, then with an arm tight around her, ran through the hole in the flames. Another rafter crashed to the floor behind them. Then they were outside.

She drew several breaths, then turned on him as if ready to bawl him out. Spotting the gelding munching grass down by the lake, she looked taken aback. "Oh, he's all right. All the horses are out," she added, spotting the others huddled together near the patio. One nibbled on the flowers planted there.

Kyle quelled the impulse either to beat her or kiss her, he wasn't sure which she deserved, and turned his attention to wetting down a tool shed in hopes of saving it.

Megan hooked up another hose and sprayed the roof of the house as sparks were carried in that direction by the breeze. Jess and Kate and Amanda arrived with Shannon and Rory right behind them.

The men took over the fight while Kate and Shannon led Megan to the patio. Shannon checked her over for injuries.

"You have a cut on the back of your head. No burns, though," she reported. She pressed a tissue to the spot.

Megan held the makeshift bandage in place. "I hit my head on something in the stable. The gelding panicked and knocked me end over teakettle." She winked at her niece, five-year-old Amanda, who worried when anyone got hurt.

"I'll get an ice pack," Shannon decided and went inside. She returned in a minute with a plastic bag of frozen broccoli. "I knew this stuff was good for something."

She cleaned the wound, then put the broccoli bag on the injury to stop the swelling.

By the time the fire trucks arrived, the stable was a smoldering husk of its former self. Bright licks of fire still burned along some rafters and support beams. None of the other buildings had burned, thanks to the diligence of the three men. In a few minutes after the firefighters took over, the fire was out.

For the rest of the afternoon, neighbors, attracted by the smoke or the radio reports, stopped by. Megan reported all she knew to the fire chief, who put his analysis team to searching through the ruins as they cooled.

Megan felt something soft on her leg. Looking down, she smiled in relief as she lifted the barn cat onto her lap. "Sorry," she whispered. "I forgot about you."

"She probably used up one of her nine lives if she was in the stable when the fire started," a masculine voice spoke behind her.

Megan would always recognize his voice, she thought. It was full of husky nuances and reminded her of twilight and low, whispered secrets barely heard above the wind in the cottonwoods—a lover's voice, warm and honey-smooth. Kyle dropped to his haunches in front of her.

"How are you?" he asked.

"Fine. A bump on the head, but nothing serious."

He inspected the wound. "It's stopped bleeding. You'll have a goose egg there for a few days."

She nodded. "Thanks for your help."

He frowned, his gaze angry as he skimmed her face. "Little fool," he said in a growl, "you could have gotten yourself killed."

"The gelding panicked," she explained. "I had to get him out."

A muscle ticked in his jaw, then he shook his head as if giving up on her ever having good sense and returned to the stable where two men picked through the ruins.

"You're a mess," Kate advised in her practical manner. "Go take a shower and change clothes. You're coming to my house for supper. Shannon, you and Rory, too."

Shannon agreed and winked at Megan. Megan managed a smile. In the bathroom, she was shocked at her appearance. There were black lashings of soot and grit all over her face and arms and clothing. Her hands were black with it. Blood had run from her hair and down one side of her neck. She could easily qualify as a monster for a horror movie.

When she laughed, she realized her throat was raw from the smoke. She stripped and hurried into the shower.

Fifteen minutes later, she felt, and looked, much better. Dressed, she dried her hair, careful of the throbbing wound on the back of her head, and put clips at the temples. When she went into the kitchen, Kate exchanged the bag of broccoli for one with peas and pearl onions and insisted she keep it on the lump. Megan didn't have the energy to argue.

Later, feeling listless, she went home with Kate and Jess and Amanda. They made her rest in the recliner while they cleaned up, then Kate put a pot roast and vegetables on the table. Rory and Shannon arrived, and dinner was served.

Megan stared uneasily at the empty place beside her when she sat down. Hearing tires crunch on the gravel outside, she tensed as they waited for the new arrival.

Kyle joined them in a minute.

''I'd hoped you could come,'' Kate said, beaming a smile on him. ''Did the firemen determine what caused the fire?''

He nodded and took the indicated place next to Megan. ''Faulty wiring in the loft. They thought mice might have gnawed the insulation off.''

"Oh," Megan said.

Everyone looked at her.

"Tabby found some mice in there. I didn't think about them bothering the wiring, though."

"You should set some traps," Amanda advised. "That's what we did."

"Well," Megan said philosophically, "I think it's a little late for that."

She surprised them all by bursting into laughter. Seeing the concern in her cousins' eyes, she stopped, then thanked them again for helping out. She was silent the rest of the meal. When everyone finished, she thanked Kate and said she'd like to go home. She wished she'd driven her own vehicle so she wouldn't have to bother them.

"I'll take you home," Kyle volunteered.

"It's out of your way."

He shrugged, obviously impatient with her remark. Megan decided that, as with her relatives, it was easier not to argue with him. She received hugs from everyone, then was sent on her way with Kyle.

As she looked at the moon, which peered at the world from behind the ridge of mountains, she felt weepy and tired. The silence bothered her. "Did you know that we'll have a Friday the thirteenth and a full moon on the same day this year?"

Kyle flicked her a curious glance. "No."

"Yes. It won't happen again for fourteen years. Then the next time is in 2056. I think," she added earnestly, not sure if she remembered it correctly.

"You're just a fount of information," he said with an odd twist to the words.

His attitude hurt her feelings and she shut up. When she sniffed, he sighed.

"Sorry," he said. "I'm still a little...tense. When I looked over at your place and saw the stable—"

He broke off and gave her another harsh glance. She wished he didn't hate her so much. She looked away.

"When I didn't see you, I thought the worst," he continued. "When I arrived, I saw I was right—you were in the midst of the flames, trying to save a damned horse that didn't have the sense to save itself."

"It wasn't mine," she explained. "It belonged to another family. I was trying to train it—"

He muttered an expletive.

She gazed out the window for the rest of the short trip. The sadness seemed overwhelming when the burned-out stable came into view. She wished...she wished things could have been different, that she and Kyle had met in another time and place, with no past between them.

If wishes were wings...

"Thank you so much for your help," she said sincerely when he stopped in front of her house. She hopped out, gave him a bright farewell smile and headed inside.

He didn't take the hint. Instead he, too, got out and followed at her heels.

At the patio door, she thanked him again. He

opened the door and ushered her inside, then closed it behind him.

"I'm really tired," she began in a polite tone.

"I am, too." He immediately took up her complaint.

She stared at him reproachfully.

"Tired of not sleeping," he continued. A smile lit his face, creating attractive creases at each side of his mouth. His gaze was watchful, almost wary.

She sighed helplessly. The stable was gone along with a third of her hay crop. The whole ranch smelled like stale smoke. The day seemed too much all of a sudden.

"Try counting sheep," she suggested with an edge to the words.

He shook his head. "I'm tired of trying not to think of you each and every moment of the day. And night."

Suddenly she couldn't breathe, couldn't think. An abyss of darkness opened inside her. She looked away.

A gentle finger under her chin lifted her face to his. "Don't you know what I'm saying?"

She shook her head. The sting of tears forced her to grit her teeth and hold on…oh, please, let her hold on until he left…

"I'm tired of trying to live without the one thing I need most of all in my life."

He paused and gave her such a somber stare she was seized by a need to comfort him. Which was ridiculous.

"I'm your enemy," she reminded him, desperate to keep distance between them, afraid she was hearing things he wasn't saying.

"Sweet enemy," he murmured. "I hope all of my enemies are like you."

He slipped his hands into her hair, and suddenly there was hardly any room between them at all, not even enough to breathe. She felt dizzy and unsure.

"Kyle—"

"Brave," he said. "Honorable. Loyal. All important qualities to share with our children."

"Children," she repeated stupidly.

"Let's start with two." He smiled into her eyes. "Then we'll decide about having more."

"More," she said. She reached into her swirling emotions and pulled one out at random. Anger. "I really don't have time for this…this…" She couldn't decide what it was. "…conversation."

"How about this?" He kissed her lightly.

It wasn't near enough. It was too much. She wanted to cling or throw a crying fit, to kiss him for an eternity or throw things. Deciding which to do first proved too much. She covered her face with both hands, afraid the tears were going to win out. She couldn't bear the humiliation of him seeing her weak and weepy.

"Don't," he murmured, concern shadowing his eyes. "I can't stand to see you hurt or unhappy."

"I'm not," she denied, then stopped as her voice failed her. She closed her eyes and shook her head. "I'm very tired," she told him.

‘‘Come on.’’

He led her into the living room and gently pushed her into one of the comfortable recliners. After pulling a hassock over, he sat at her feet.

‘‘Megan Rose Windom,’’ he said, taking her hand. ‘‘Will you do me the great honor of marrying me and ending my sleepless bachelor nights?’’

‘‘You’re a Herriot,’’ she reminded him.

‘‘Your enemy.’’ He gazed at her tenderly.

She shook her head. ‘‘Not mine. Yours. My family—’’

He laid a finger over her lips. ‘‘Don’t you think it’s time we truly buried the past?’’

‘‘Can we?’’ Hope leaped into her heart. She ruthlessly pushed it aside. ‘‘There’s such a long history between us. I couldn’t bear it if you hated…’’ She stopped, fearing she’d given too much away.

Kyle experienced an ache deep down inside where only this woman had ever reached. ‘‘How could I hate the person who possesses my whole heart? I love you, Megan Rose. Can you, will you, accept that?’’

Staring into his eyes, she saw truth and tenderness and caring. Like a storm cloud parting, a bright warmth sprang into being inside her. She touched his face with something like astonishment.

‘‘You’re serious,’’ she said in wonder.

‘‘Never more so in my life.’’

‘‘Your mother—’’

‘‘Is ready to move on with her life,’’ he told her.

"She's accepted what happened and, I think, gotten past it. She knows how I feel."

"About us?"

"Yes. That leaves only one person to consider." He paused. "You. I want to build a life with you, one of sunshine, not shadows."

She suddenly knew what he was asking. He wanted to be done with the past entirely. He wanted a future without doubts or anger or hatred between them.

"I don't have nightmares anymore," she said slowly. "The child who haunted my dreams with her fears is gone. I said farewell to her a month ago. Our last night..." Tears filled her eyes and she stopped.

Kyle brushed the tears from her lashes. "She had a right to weep, that little girl. She suffered more than children ought to. I think we can promise something better for our kids, don't you?"

She nodded.

"Marry me?" he said.

"Yes."

He lifted her and settled into the chair with her across his lap. "I feel as if I've been on a long and perilous journey and finally, finally found my haven. My heart's home. You."

She laid her head on his shoulder and felt his heart beating in rhythm with hers. She sensed his strength. More, she sensed his love. Like the force hidden at the heart of the earth, it was unseen but powerful. Absolute. A thing she could depend on.

The brightness grew, lighting the world even as

the last rays of twilight slipped beyond the horizon. From the cottonwoods, a raven cawed sleepily, calling others to come in from the dark.

"The ravens," she murmured.

"They'll bring us nothing but good luck," Kyle averred. "The Windraven legacy will be one of happiness from now on."

They sealed the promise with a kiss.

Chapter Fourteen

"Careful," Kyle said.

He was talking to his mother. He held her arm and made sure she stepped out of the sailboat onto the granite island with no problem.

Megan, too, watched with a new parent's anxiety over her firstborn. Joan settled in the chair Kyle positioned for her, her gaze on her granddaughter, three-month-old Willow Rose Herriot.

"Here, honey." Kyle offered his arm to Megan. But when she would have stepped onto the gangplank, he swept her into his arms and spun her around. "Happy birthday," he murmured and gave her a kiss.

A chorus of best wishes from her cousins, their husbands and the other two kids, Jeremy and Amanda, followed. Megan beamed at them.

She nursed the baby while Joan, Kate and Shannon spread out a special picnic lunch, complete with cake and ice cream, on a flat spot. Kate called her kids, who were exploring a tiny pool in the rocks.

"This is a beautiful spot," Joan said. "Why don't I hold the baby while you eat, Megan?"

Kyle laughed. "She's hardly put her down since she was born. Talk about spoiled." He gave his mom a mock-frown, then grinned.

Glancing over at his wife of almost two years, he felt contentment flow through him like a deep, quiet river. They lived in the Herriot house and were renovating the old Windom mansion into a bed-and-breakfast operation. With a contract from a sports outfitter, plus a campground, they would have the cash income necessary to keep a spread that size going.

Life was good.

Megan caught Kyle's eyes on her and smiled. She liked the way he looked at her, so full of love and happiness it gleamed from his eyes and brightened the whole world.

Checking her mother-in-law, she saw the rocky island held no bad memories for her. While Joan had never treated her with less than warmth and courtesy, Megan thought the birth of Willow was the seal on their future. The past was truly gone, receding into memories of happier times as grief should.

Glancing at Kate and Jess, she felt her heart squeeze tight with love for them. Jess was her uncle, and she sometimes teased her cousin by calling her Auntie Kate.

They had debated having their children call the three older cousins by honorary aunt and uncle titles, then had decided they didn't need to claim a closer kinship. Love was the binding that held them together, not just blood.

Rory hovered over Shannon these days. And well he should. She was expecting their first child within a month and was as big as a cow. Megan and Kate suspected twins, but the couple wasn't telling.

Not that it mattered. However many Shannon had, they would be welcomed into the family with delight.

Love had no boundaries, Megan had learned. Neither a lake nor a tragedy could keep apart those who were destined to fall in love.

Jeremy and Amanda bounded up, grabbed their plates and chose two boulders to perch on. Their laughter brought smiles to the adults as they argued over who could eat the biggest piece of cake.

She gave the drowsy Willow to her grandma. It was, she thought, the very best of times.

* * * * *

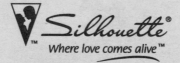

HARLEQUIN "SILHOUETTE MAKES YOU A STAR!" CONTEST 1308
OFFICIAL RULES
NO PURCHASE NECESSARY TO ENTER

1. To enter, follow directions published in the offer to which you are responding. Contest begins June 1, 2001, and ends on September 28, 2001. Entries must be postmarked by September 28, 2001, and received by October 5, 2001. Enter by hand-printing (or typing) on an 8 ½" x 11" piece of paper your name, address (including zip code), contest number/name and attaching a script containing 500 words or less, along with drawings, photographs or magazine cutouts, or combinations thereof (i.e., collage) on no larger than 9" x 12" piece of paper, describing how the Silhouette books make romance come alive for you. Mail via first-class mail to: Harlequin "Silhouette Makes You a Star!" Contest 1308, (in the U.S.) P.O. Box 9069, Buffalo, NY 14269-9069, (in Canada) P.O. Box 637, Fort Erie, Ontario, Canada L2A 5X3. Limit one entry per person, household or organization.

2. Contests will be judged by a panel of members of the Harlequin editorial, marketing and public relations staff. Fifty percent of criteria will be judged against script and fifty percent will be judged against drawing, photographs and/or magazine cutouts. Judging criteria will be based on the following:

   - Sincerity—25%
   - Originality and Creativity—50%
   - Emotionally Compelling—25%

   In the event of a tie, duplicate prizes will be awarded. Decisions of the judges are final.

3. All entries become the property of Torstar Corp. and may be used for future promotional purposes. Entries will not be returned. No responsibility is assumed for lost, late, illegible, incomplete, inaccurate, nondelivered or misdirected mail.

4. Contest open only to residents of the U.S. (except Puerto Rico) and Canada who are 18 years of age or older, and is void wherever prohibited by law; all applicable laws and regulations apply. Any litigation within the Province of Quebec respecting the conduct or organization of a publicity contest may be submitted to the Régie des alcools, des courses et des jeux for a ruling. Any litigation respecting the awarding of a prize may be submitted to the Régie des alcools, des courses et des jeux only for the purpose of helping the parties reach a settlement. Employees and immediate family members of Torstar Corp. and D. L. Blair, Inc., their affiliates, subsidiaries and all other agencies, entities and persons connected with the use, marketing or conduct of this contest are not eligible to enter. Taxes on prizes are the sole responsibility of the winner. Acceptance of any prize offered constitutes permission to use winner's name, photograph or other likeness for the purposes of advertising, trade and promotion on behalf of Torstar Corp., its affiliates and subsidiaries without further compensation to the winner, unless prohibited by law.

5. Winner will be determined no later than November 30, 2001, and will be notified by mail. Winner will be required to sign and return an Affidavit of Eligibility/Release of Liability/Publicity Release form within 15 days after winner notification. Noncompliance within that time period may result in disqualification and an alternative winner may be selected. All travelers must execute a Release of Liability prior to ticketing and must possess required travel documents (e.g., passport, photo ID) where applicable. Trip must be booked by December 31, 2001, and completed within one year of notification. No substitution of prize permitted by winner. Torstar Corp. and D. L. Blair, Inc., their parents, affiliates and subsidiaries are not responsible for errors in printing of contest, entries and/or game pieces. In the event of printing or other errors that may result in unintended prize values or duplication of prizes, all affected game pieces or entries shall be null and void. **Purchase or acceptance of a product offer does not improve your chances of winning.**

6. Prizes: (1) Grand Prize—A 2-night/3-day trip for two (2) to New York City, including round-trip coach air transportation nearest winner's home and hotel accommodations (double occupancy) at The Plaza Hotel, a glamorous afternoon makeover at a trendy New York spa, $1,000 in U.S. spending money and an opportunity to have a professional photo taken and appear in a Silhouette advertisement (approximate retail value: $7,000). (10) Ten Runner-Up Prizes of gift packages (retail value $50 ea.). Prizes consist of only those items listed as part of the prize. Limit one prize per person. Prize is valued in U.S. currency.

7. For the name of the winner (available after December 31, 2001) send a self-addressed, stamped envelope to: Harlequin "Silhouette Makes You a Star!" Contest 1197 Winners, P.O. Box 4200 Blair, NE 68009-4200 or you may access the www.eHarlequin.com Web site through February 28, 2002.

Contest sponsored by Torstar Corp., P.O Box 9042, Buffalo, NY 14269-9042.

SRMYAS2

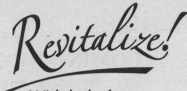

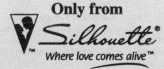

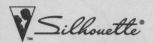

COMING NEXT MONTH

#1423 THE MARRIAGE CONSPIRACY—Christine Rimmer
Conveniently Yours
Single mom Joleen Tilly married her best friend, Dekker Smith—aka Russell Bravo—heir to the Bravo fortune, strictly to keep custody of her son. But once under the same roof, this couple found it impossible to sleep in separate beds. Now Dekker must decide if his heart, once destroyed by love, could ever heal again….

#1424 DATELINE MATRIMONY—Gina Wilkins
Hot Off the Press
Each morning waitress Teresa Scott served breakfast to reporter Riley O'Neal, but he wanted more than a refill of coffee—*he wanted her.* A working woman with responsibilities, she had no time for no-strings fun. Then a scandalous news story had them teaming up together and hoping that it would end happily ever after….

#1425 THE TRUTH ABOUT TATE—Marilyn Pappano
Tate Rawlins would do anything to protect his family. So when journalist Natalie Grant threatened to expose his illegitimate half brother, the rancher took on his brother's identity. But when he fell in love with the enemy, was the only thing that stood between them the truth about Tate?

#1426 HIS LITTLE GIRL'S LAUGHTER—Karen Rose Smith
Rafe Pierson's little girl hadn't uttered a word since her mother's death, so the devoted single father sought out psychologist Shannon Collins for help. But when the lovely doctor turned his daughter's frown into laughter once more, would Rafe realize that he also needed Shannon…for a lifetime?

#1427 THE WOMAN FOR DUSTY CONRAD—Tori Carrington
Dusty was back in town to get a divorce from his former wife, feisty firefighter Jolie Conrad…whom he'd once believed was the only woman for him. But when a fire flared, he was right by Jolie's side. Would this long-burning blaze become the torch that lit their way into each other's arms again?

#1428 COWGIRL BE MINE—Elaine Nichols
A Woman's Way
Ten years ago, cowgirl Mandy Thomson trampled Jake Miller's heart. Now she was faced with the painful aftermath of a devastating bull riding accident. But when she found herself living under the same roof as Jake, could he heal her wounded pride, and she—her lover's heart?

SSECNM0901